FIREFLY HOLLOW

ALISON McGHEE
ILLUSTRATED BY CHRISTOPHER DENISE

A Caitlyn Dlouhy Book

Atheneum Books for Young Readers
New York   London   Toronto   Sydney   New Delhi

Acknowledgments

This book would not have been possible were it up to me alone. Thanks to Christopher Denise, for his beautiful artwork; Julie Schumacher and Kathi Appelt, for their insightful suggestions; Raquel Briskin Counihan, for the loan of her peaceful lakeside writing retreat; and Holly McGhee, for her unflagging support. Finally, deepest thanks to the lovely Caitlyn Dlouhy, whose editing skills were, and are always, invaluable. —A. M.

atheneum

ATHENEUM BOOKS FOR YOUNG READERS • An imprint of Simon & Schuster Children's Publishing Division • 1230 Avenue of the Americas, New York, New York 10020 • This book is a work of fiction. Any references to historical events, real people, or real places are used fictitiously. Other names, characters, places, and events are products of the author's imagination, and any resemblance to actual events or places or persons, living or dead, is entirely coincidental. • Text copyright © 2015 by Alison McGhee • Illustrations copyright © 2015 by Christopher Denise • All rights reserved, including the right of reproduction in whole or in part in any form. • ATHENEUM BOOKS FOR YOUNG READERS is a registered trademark of Simon & Schuster, Inc. Atheneum logo is a trademark of Simon & Schuster, Inc. • For information about special discounts for bulk purchases, please contact Simon & Schuster Special Sales at 1-866-506-1949 or business@simonandschuster.com. • The Simon & Schuster Speakers Bureau can bring authors to your live event. For more information or to book an event, contact the Simon & Schuster Speakers Bureau at 1-866-248-3049 or visit our website at www.simonspeakers.com. • Also available in an Atheneum Books for Young Readers hardcover edition • Book design by Sonia Chaghatzbanian • The text for this book was set in Horley Old Style and Aged. • Manufactured in China • 0517 SCP • First Atheneum Books for Young Readers paperback edition August 2016 • 10 9 8 7 6 5 4 3 • The Library of Congress has cataloged the hardcover edition as follows: • McGhee, Alison, 1960– • Firefly hollow / Alison McGhee ; illustrated by Christopher Denise.—1st ed.• p. cm. • Summary: Because their dreams of daring adventures go against the cautious teachings of their nations, Firefly and Cricket set out on their own, find a home with kindly Vole, and together help a grieving "miniature giant" named Peter. • ISBN 978-1-4424-2336-7 (hc) • ISBN 978-1-4424-9812-9 (eBook) • ISBN 978-1-4424-2337-4 (pbk) • [1. Fireflies—Fiction. 2. Crickets—Fiction. 3. Voles—Fiction. 4. Friendship—Fiction. 5. Adventure and adventurers—Fiction. 6. Grief—Fiction.] • I. Denise, Christopher, ill. II. Title. • PZ7.M4784675Fir 2014 • [Fic]—dc23   2013004705

For Kathi Appelt

—A. M.

For my friend Brian Jacques—

Airíonn muid uainn thú

—C. D.

CONTENTS

CHAPTER ONE

I COULD FLY THAT HIGH?

S *woop!*

Firefly flitted through a knothole in the hollow tree, straight out into the clearing and straight back in again. The night air outside the hollow tree was cool, and the air inside was warm. She whooshed back and forth from cool to warm, outside to inside, faster and faster and faster until—*yikes*—she accidentally side-swiped Elder.

"Whoa!" he said. "Watch where you're going there, Firefly."

His tone was stern. But when no one else was looking, he blinked their secret code at her: three fast and two long.

"Sorry, Elder," said Firefly, and she blinked the secret code back.

Most of the other elders viewed Firefly as slightly crazy and a clear threat to the safety and well-being of the youth of the firefly nation, but not Elder. He had been her hero since the night when she, as a one-centimeter-round baby, long before it was time to learn to fly, rolled right out of her spiderweb hammock and flung herself off the edge of her cubby.

"Careful there, little one," Elder had said, swooping underneath her just in time.

"Yeehaw!" she had yelled. "Higher! Higher!"

And she had waved with one wing to the other baby fireflies, who were gaping from their spiderweb hammocks, as Elder piggybacked her around and around the inside of the hollow tree. He finally returned her to her cubby and tucked her in, pulling the milkweed blanket up to her chin.

"Will you teach me how to fly by myself, Elder?" she had whispered.

"Soon," he had said. "When the time is right."

"But I want to learn *now*."

"Soon," said Elder again, and he smiled.

"*Promise?*"

"Promise."

Before she fell asleep that night, she turned her head so that she could look out the knothole into the dark night sky. There were the moon and the stars, shining high above.

"They're so beautiful," she whispered.

"That they are," agreed Elder. "But don't let the others hear you say that."

And he blinked an hypnotic pattern to lull her into sleep.

Elder kept his promise. Eventually she and all the others learned to fly. None of the other little fireflies flew as well as Firefly did, but at least they flew.

Firefly spread her wings now and zipped back outside. She loved the feel of the wind whooshing her up into the air. Imagine if she had to plod along the creature path on her spindly legs. Imagine not being able to fly, when flying was all she had ever wanted to do!

Midair flips, loop-de-loops, figure eights—all these were moves she had made up and practiced, at first in a corner of the clearing with Elder hovering nearby, ready to catch her if she fell, and then right in front of the others. The other little fireflies were too scared to try. Rules had been drummed into them in Air Safety class since they were tiny: Don't fly beyond the clearing; don't fly higher than the first big branch of the white pine; don't fly in the rain.

There was Air Safety class, and there was Basics of Blinking class, in which the baby fireflies learned how to signal left, right, straight, and right of way. But nothing compared to Fear of Giants class. All small fireflies were required to recite the three Fundamental Rules of Giants at the start and end of every class.

1. Giants are to be feared.
2. Giants are the enemies of the firefly nation.
3. Giants are to be avoided at all costs.

But it was hard to avoid giants entirely, because three of them lived in Firefly Hollow, in a house at the bend of the river: mother giant, father giant, and the miniature giant they called Peter. That was how it was done in their world—miniature ones lived with their parents in houses separate from other giants—unlike young and elder fireflies, who all lived in the same hollow tree, sharing their cubbies and eating their snails together. The mother and father giants were dreadful creatures. When they tromped about, their enormous weight shook the very earth.

TROMP. TROMP. TROMP.

"The giants are out!" the young fireflies would shout to one another when they were playing Death by Giant. *"Flee!"*

Something else that all the fireflies lived in fear of was the Jar.

The Jar was kept in a special roped-off corner at the Museum of Giant Artifacts, just down the trail from the neighboring School for Young Crickets. The museum held objects that had washed ashore from the giant nation:

A blue knife with a terrifying serrated edge.

A spool of yellow thread, thread that could be used for any number of evil purposes.

A huge red shoe, which, if tromped down on a resting firefly, would mean certain death.

These were just a few of the items in the Museum of Giant Artifacts. There were sections devoted to various other terrors of the giant world, among them games.

Games with names like baseball and basketball and kickball and soccer, games with balls that could roll right over a resting firefly and crush it dead then and there.

But it was the Jar that was especially horrifying to the firefly nation. The Jar! It contained actual firefly corpses! Once viewed, the Jar could never be forgotten.

"This is what will happen if you ever get too close to a giant," the elders said, pointing with one wing at the dreadful object.

Oh, the poor lost fireflies who had met their end inside that jar. What a hideous fate: caught in midflight by giants, giants with their long legs and their reaching arms and their glass jars with the holes punched in the lids. The Museum of Giant Artifacts filled with screams during this portion of every field trip, screams so loud that they drowned out the constant, robotic chirping from the School for Young Crickets.

Despite the shrieks, the elders hovered grimly. The

young ones had to learn what would happen if they got too close to a giant. *Giants are the enemies of the firefly nation.* All it took was one visit to the museum, and all the young fireflies accepted the wisdom of the elders: Stay far, far away from the giants.

All but Firefly.

The truth of it was, giants fascinated her. Unbeknownst to anyone but Elder, she sometimes snuck out of the clearing to spy on the miniature giant, the one called Peter. At first she spied on him playing catch with another miniature giant. The other miniature giant was gone now, but Firefly still spied on Peter from afar, as he sat on the sand or perched in the branches of a white birch by the water.

Was he *really* that terrifying?

Secretly, Firefly thought that there was a lot to admire about giants. They were the ones who had invented spaceships that flew them to outer space—poor wing-less creatures that they were—and Firefly loved outer space. Sometimes, when she was out practicing her aerial maneuvers, she turned on her back and stared up. The vast darkness held the moon and the stars.

When she was tiny, Elder used to sneak her outside after bedtime, so that they could look up at the night sky together.

"Are you sure the stars are really that far away, Elder?"

"I'm sure."

There were thousands of them, tiny pinpoints of light, shimmering down on the two of them as they hovered on their backs in the clearing. They didn't look *that* far away to Firefly.

"Double sure? Triple sure?"

"Quadruple sure."

Firefly sighed. She lay on her back for a while, fluttering her wings just enough to stay aloft. She had a question for Elder, a question that she was scared to ask. Gradually, she worked up her courage.

"Elder?"

"Yes?"

"What if you were a little firefly, and you, you . . ."
She trailed off.

"You what?" he prompted her.

"You wanted to see what it was like beyond Firefly Hollow."

There. She had said it. She wanted to know what it was like beyond Firefly Hollow, something that went against every rule of the firefly nation.

"Are *you* that little firefly?" Elder said.

She looked around to make sure that they were the only ones out, then nodded.

"Well," said Elder, "I'm going to tell you a secret."

He floated close so he could whisper in her ear. "Maybe someday you'll get a chance to see."

"Really? When?"

"When it's time."

Argh! That was Elder's answer to everything.

"How about now, Elder? Right now!"

Elder just smiled and shook his head. He blinked their

secret code—three fast, two long—a code that could mean any number of things, such as *Are you hungry?* Or *Do you want to sneak out and practice aerial maneuvers?* Or *Want to come look at the stars with me?* but in this case meant *I know you want to go right now, but you have to be patient.* Firefly turned over on her stomach and tried to ignore him. Elder kept on blinking, though, and eventually she blinked back.

But when she returned to her spiderweb hammock, Firefly thought about it some more. If someday she was really going to fly beyond Firefly Hollow, then she would need to build up her strength. That was something she could work on right now, wasn't it? So she practiced her aerial maneuvers over and over, over and over, hoping that one day they would come in handy. And she timed herself for nonstop flying. Her best time so far was three hours, twelve minutes, and seven seconds. Without one single break.

Swoop!

"Firefly!"

"Firefly!"

"Firefly!"

Her friends were gathered by the lowest branch of the white pine that stood in the center of the clearing, waiting for her.

Firefly spread her wings, did one of her famous loop-de-loops, and landed in their midst. Around and around the white pine they flew, sparkling and blinking. The moon hung round and yellow, and the night sky shimmered with light from the stars.

"Imagine flying up that high," said Firefly, pointing with one wing.

"Are you kidding?" said one.

"No, thank you," said another.

"I'll stay right here in the clearing," said a third.

"The giants flew up there, you know," said Firefly. "Straight up to the moon."

Giants? All around her tiny firefly bodies shuddered in midair at the very sound of the dreaded word. Firefly ignored them.

"Imagine walking around on the moon," she said, "the way the giants did."

That did it. The very idea of walking on the moon was so shocking that—*THUD*—one of them forgot to keep his wings in motion and fell right out of the air. Good thing the pine needle floor of the forest was soft. The fallen one shook his wings and hauled himself back up through the air to the first branch.

"Fireflies aren't even supposed to go beyond the clearing," he said.

"We're not supposed to fly any higher than the first big branch," said another.

"We're never, *ever* supposed to fly beyond Firefly Hollow," said a third.

"I know," said Firefly. "But the giants did."

Thud.

Another one down. The air vibrated with worried wings and firefly shrieks.

"Just imagine it," said Firefly, spinning up and around the rest of them. "Just imagine looking down on Firefly Hollow from outer space."

"No!"

"No!"

"No!"

Yes, thought Firefly. Sometimes it was fun to shock them.

On that night, after her tired friends returned to their cubbies in the hollow tree, Firefly stayed outside. She flipped onto her back and hovered in midair, looking up at the moon. Cricket music rose all around her. Since they were young, girl crickets set the beat and boy crickets stroked their serrated wings against each other, chirping songs about marsh grass waving in the wind, and white puffs of dandelions, and pine needles on the forest floor. These were the things that crickets always sang about. Nice, but boring.

Why don't they sing about the moon? thought Firefly. *Or*

the stars? Or flying? Or something *exciting, like . . . giants?*

But none of them did. The young crickets were just like the young fireflies, thought Firefly, feeling cross. They too were afraid of everything beyond Firefly Hollow. She raised her wings high, ready to return to her spiderweb hammock.

But wait.

What was that?

A single cricket out there was singing a song she had never before heard any cricket sing. She flitted to the left side of the clearing, then to the right, trying to be sure she had really heard what she thought she'd heard. Was that it? Over there on the far, far left? There—yes! There it was.

"Take me out to the ball game
Take me out with the crowd."

This was not a typical cricket song!
Firefly floated closer.

"Buy me some peanuts . . ."

Wow.

This cricket had a beautiful voice. He was singing alone.

"and Cracker Jack . . ."

Firefly floated closer still. This song was not a cricket song at all. Firefly could hardly believe it, but this song was, in fact, a giant song. It was the same song that the miniature giant used to sing, back in the days when his friend was still there and they played catch on the shore.

"I don't care . . ."

This was a song about forbidden things: giants and ball games and crowds. Firefly fluttered her wings just enough to stay aloft, trying to be as quiet as possible, so that she wouldn't disturb the unknown cricket and his song.

". . . if I never get back."

Somewhere out there was a cricket who snuck off at night to sing about something forbidden, something dangerous, something that none of the other crickets wanted. Somewhere out there was a

    cricket

        like

            her.

CHAPTER TWO

IF CRICKETS COULD CATCH

Cricket lived down the path from Firefly's hollow tree. He was one of many students in Teacher's class at the School for Young Crickets, where the walls were made of twigs and the roof was made of leaves and the floor was smooth dried mud.

Teacher taught all three classes considered essential for the proper education of a young cricket:

1. Telling Temperature

2. High Jumping

3. Fear of Giants

She hopped about sternly during Telling Temperature class, one wing counting out the seconds against her leg.

One, two, three.

She hopped about equally sternly in High Jumping class, inspecting each and every student for proper height, speed, and quality of leap.

The young crickets followed her lead in everything. All of them, that is, except for Cricket and his one friend, Gloria with the blue-green eyes, who sat by herself in the far corner. Cricket was good at Telling Temperature and High Jumping. But he was bad at Fear of Giants, and Teacher—who was strict and keen-eyed—knew it.

This very evening, she had called the young crickets together for a refresher course in danger, meant especially for Cricket. They gathered together on the outskirts of Firefly Hollow, not far from the clearing where the young fireflies were beginning to emerge from their hollow tree.

"Time for review," said Teacher. "Name the three greatest threats to a cricket's life."

"Water," said a little brown cricket.

"Correct," said Teacher. "Water is to be feared."

"All water?" said another cricket, an especially young one. "Even a teeny little bit of water?"

"*All* water," said Teacher. "The river, the sea, even rain. Crickets have been known to drown in mud puddles. Even a heavy drenching is dangerous, because it can crush your carapace."

The young crickets looked anxiously up at the sky. *Rain*, thought Cricket. Could rain really be that bad? It looked so pretty when it came pattering down onto the trail and the leaves and the grass.

"If ever you find yourself outside in the rain," said Teacher, "what should you do?"

"Flee!" said a skinny, long-legged cricket. "Flee before a drop crushes your carapace!"

"Very good," said Teacher. "Name another great threat to a cricket's life."

"Sun," said a plump green cricket.

"Correct," said Teacher. "An excess of sun is a terrible thing. Too wet, and a cricket can drown. Too dry, and a carapace can crack. If ever you find yourself outside in the hot sun, what should you do?"

"Flee!" said another cricket. "Flee before you dry up and die!"

"Very good," said Teacher.

She reared back on her hind legs and waved an arm in the air to emphasize her point, which was that the world was a dangerous place. The rain, the sun, the water, the woods with its creatures of prey, just waiting for a tasty morsel of young cricket.

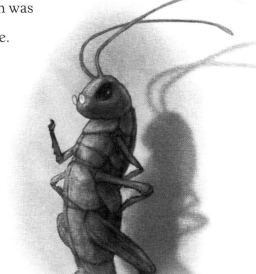

"But what, my little crickets, is the greatest threat of all?"

Teacher swept her gaze over the massed young crickets, waiting for them to give the answer, which everyone already knew:

"Giants."

Cricket was the only one who stayed silent.

"Very good," said Teacher, nodding. "Very good. And why are giants the greatest threat of all?"

She looked directly at Cricket, as if this question was meant for him alone.

"They don't see us," chanted the young crickets.

"And what else?"

"They don't hear us."

"And what else?"

"Stomp! Tromp! Aaargh!"

And the crowd of young crickets keeled over on their carapaces, all six legs waving feebly in the air, pretending to be in mortal pain from a giant's misplaced footstep. Death by Giants was their favorite part of class.

Cricket looked at his classmates, writhing and wiggling on their backs. Laughing. Teacher leaped about grimly, a stern expression on her face.

"Stay far, far away," she called, raising her voice above the fake groans and moans of her students. "Giants are the enemies of the cricket nation."

Eventually the little crickets rolled one another back upright. They straightened up and quieted down and nodded: *Stay far, far away from the giants.* But Cricket gathered his courage and asked a question.

"Are *all* giants bad?" he said. "Aren't there *any* good ones?"

The other young crickets raised their heads, astonished and annoyed. They gazed at him with dark, silent stares. Just when they were having so much fun playing Death by Giant, Cricket had to go and ask one of his questions. Why did he always have to do that? Of course all giants were bad! Of course there were no good giants! Didn't he *ever* listen to Teacher? The little crickets rolled their eyes at one another.

Teacher sighed. She gave him a look that Cricket recognized. It was a look that told him to be quiet, to stop asking questions, to listen to her for once. Cricket knew that Teacher was sick of his constant questions, but he couldn't help asking them. Now he waited patiently, hoping that she would answer.

"You've seen the giants, haven't you, Cricket?" she finally said.

He nodded. Yes, he had seen the giants. Along with the other young crickets, the elders had taken him on a field trip to the edge of the woods, near the giants' house. They had all perched by the marsh grass and observed them playing catch. The father giant and the mother giant were, admittedly, horrifying creatures, loud and clumsy, crashing about and shaking the earth.

But the miniature giant, the one they called Peter, didn't seem so awful.

So what if he was huge? He wasn't mean, as far as Cricket could tell. So what if he had missed when playing catch one day, so that his baseball came whipping over the heads of the crickets and they had all fled back to the safety of the school and vowed never to get that close to a giant again? At least Peter was trying to learn something new. He was practicing. Wasn't that how you got better at something?

In Cricket's opinion, it would only be a good thing if crickets knew how to catch falling objects. Then maybe they wouldn't have to live in mortal fear of rain, let alone errant baseballs.

But truth be told, that one school field trip hadn't been the only time Cricket had spied on the giants. In fact, Cricket had kept count of the number of times he had snuck back down to the sand while the others were asleep, to spy on Peter from the safety of the reeds, and the count was up to forty-seven.

Yes, forty-seven.

Forty-seven was a higher number than Cricket had ever heard any other cricket, including Teacher, count to. He was amazed that he could even count that high. But practice made perfect, didn't it? And by now Cricket was well practiced in the arts of both spying and counting.

Back when the miniature giant's friend was still around, Cricket would clap his wings together if one of them made a particularly good catch. He had memorized the song they used to sing together, a wonderful song about baseball and peanuts and never getting back. The lives of the miniature giants—their freedom, their laughter, their huge baseballs and even huger mitts—fascinated Cricket.

"You've seen the giants, Cricket," Teacher was saying now. She stood above him, her wing waving back and forth like a metronome, all the students watching. "You know how terrifying they are. And you still have to ask if they're all bad?"

She was fearsome, but Cricket didn't back down.

"Peter doesn't look so bad," he said.

Teacher rose up in agitation.

"Don't call him Peter," she growled, waving her feelers and her front legs in his direction.

"But that's his name."

"He's a miniature giant. And a miniature giant is nothing but a future giant."

"Yeah!" said the other little crickets in unison, wanting to stay in Teacher's good graces. "A miniature giant is nothing but a future giant!"

Teacher raised her wing, and the little crickets instantly quieted down.

"Tell me, Cricket," she said. "Have you or have you not learned anything from Gloria? One lollipop stick flung carelessly from the hand of a miniature giant and now there she is—one front leg and one wing permanently damaged."

Cricket nodded. He in fact wondered what she was doing at that very moment, as she couldn't join them at the edge of the hollow.

"And have you or have you not been to the Museum of Giant Artifacts?" said Teacher.

"I have," said Cricket.

"He has," said the other crickets, trying again to impress Teacher.

All of them had been to the Museum of Giant Artifacts. The young crickets hated the museum, filled as it was with objects of doom, and they dreaded their enforced visits to it. All except Cricket, that is. Once again he plucked up his courage and faced Teacher.

"If crickets knew how to catch flying objects," he said, "maybe someone could have caught that lollipop stick before it hurt Gloria."

The other crickets gasped. *Catch it? A lollipop stick? Cricket was crazy!*

"Catching a flying object is *far* beyond the capabilities of any member of the cricket nation," said Teacher. "Put that notion out of your head immediately."

But Cricket didn't.

Instead he snuck off to the museum whenever he could and went straight to the baseball section. There was a card there that showed a smiling giant crouched in the dirt, a cage over his face and a baseball mitt held up in the air. This giant was named Yogi Berra. He was the greatest catcher of the major leagues, and there was no ball, no matter how fast, no matter how difficult to catch, that Yogi Berra couldn't handle.

Cricket wanted to be the cricket version of Yogi Berra.

If I had caught that lollipop stick, he thought, *Gloria wouldn't have gotten hurt.*

Why shouldn't crickets learn how to catch flying objects? Wouldn't that make them all safer? Telling Temperature. High Jumping. Fear of Giants. And Catch for Crickets.

But none of the other crickets felt the same way. And that was why, night after night, Cricket snuck away to the riverbank, to sing the baseball song alone.

CHAPTER THREE

THE LAST OF THE LEGENDARY RIVER VOLES

Vole also lived in Firefly Hollow.

All the small creatures of the land and the air knew him, or knew of him, but none knew him well. Unlike the fireflies and the crickets, Vole was a creature of the water. He lived on a boat by the riverbank, at the base of an old white birch not far from Firefly's hollow tree. A clump of tiger lilies hid the boat in the warm months, and snow and ice kept it camouflaged in the winter.

You see, Vole was a river vole. River voles didn't live in the meadows or underground in burrows like ordinary voles. River voles were brave and adventuresome creatures, who sailed the river their whole lives long.

But long ago, when Vole was still small, the giants who lived upstream had struck down a beaver dam. This caused the river to rise up in fury, swamping the fishing boats of the river voles and sweeping both boats and voles downriver, never to be seen again. All except one. Vole.

Vole was the last of his kind, the keeper of memories.

Many summers had passed since that tragedy, summers filled with the light and music of fireflies and crickets. Many winters had also passed, winters when the little creatures slept their long sleeps and Vole fished through a hole he bored in the ice.

Vole's grandfather, a legendary river vole, had built the boat with his own paws. Curves of polished cedar ran the length and breadth of the old boat, and its mast was straight and true.

When he was young, Vole had watched his grandfather lean over the boat's railing and gather the fishing net together, paw over paw, slowly hauling in the catch. All manner of fish came swimming up in his grandfather's net, flopping and wriggling, a rainbow shimmer of scales, bright eyes casting about in fear, fins working wildly to find water that wasn't there anymore.

Vole's grandfather had begun teaching him the ancient lore of the river vole nation. He taught him to bow his head and put his paws together in honor of the fish who sustained them. He taught him to choose first one, then two, then another fish and place them in a wooden bucket filled with water. He showed Vole how to gather the net together again and fling it back over the side of the boat, letting the other fish go.

Once in the water, the fish shivered their fins and flicked their tails and were gone.

"Will we ever see them again, Grampa?"

"Maybe," his grandfather had told him. "Maybe we'll

see them again when you learn to sail. Maybe we'll catch a glimpse of them where the river meets the sea. You never know."

Vole's grandfather had been fearless. He had seen the great waters beyond, and he had stories to tell of it.

"Soon you'll see it for yourself, Vole," he had said. "You can't imagine how beautiful it is."

"When, Grampa? When?"

"When you're ready, that's when."

"But when will that be?"

His grandfather had laughed.

"You'll know when the time is right," he said.

If his grandfather had lived, he would have taught Vole everything he needed to know in order to live the true life of a river vole. In fact, he'd already begun teaching Vole how to tie sailor knots. On that tragic day, his grandfather had just finished tying a series of knots for Vole, one after another on different lengths of rope. Then he had hung them on a row of hooks in the living room and begun with the very first knot.

"This is a bowline," he had said, his paws nimbly threading one length of twine in and around another. "When in doubt, use a bowline. That's my first sailing lesson to you, little Vole."

Vole's grandfather had been afraid of nothing except the giants. Rightly so, it turned out, because when the giants ripped out the beaver dam just a few hours later, Vole's grandfather and all the other river voles who were out fishing had been lost to the wild water.

And ever since that day, Vole had been teaching himself how to sail.

He studied the *River Vole's Guide*, in which famous sailors of the past had drawn navigational diagrams and constellations, the better to understand the movement of the river and the influence of the tides. He studied the knots his grandfather had tied, matching them to the knots in the *River Vole's Guide*, undoing them and retying them. What would have taken only a few years, had the

river vole nation survived, had taken Vole a lifetime.

But he was determined. The day would come when he untied the boat from its mooring and set sail. The day would come when he, Vole, would fulfill his river vole destiny. He tried not to think about the fact that he would be alone, with no one to witness his voyage and no one waiting for him with a celebration far down-stream, where the river met the sea. That was just the way it was.

Now the sun went down, and the clearing in the woods began to glow with fireflies. Vole watched the little rebel cricket hop down the creature path and hide himself in the reeds by the riverbank. Every time Vole heard this particular cricket's song, he crept out onto his deck to listen. There was something about the little cricket and his song that made him dream of faraway places. Of what he himself might see, when he finally sailed downstream and beheld the great waters beyond.

Vole sat down on his deck chair, picked up his twine,

and practiced his clove hitch. This was a difficult knot, one that he still hadn't quite mastered. Would he ever know everything he needed to know?

"You'll know when the time is right," he reminded himself, remembering his grandfather's words. He sat on the deck and listened to the little cricket's song.

"Take me out to the ball game
Take me out with the crowd."

CHAPTER FOUR

IN SEARCH OF A CRICKET

T he sky glowed with the light from a thousand stars. It was late, later than late, the time when young fireflies began to return to the hollow tree. All night long they twirled and spun in the blackness, and now they were tired. First one, then another, and then another slipped back through the knothole. They headed straight to the snail cupboard to eat their fill before they settled into their spiderweb hammocks to sleep.

Not Firefly. She hung back, hovering in midair, thinking about that one cricket out there, the one she had heard earlier that evening, singing the giant's baseball song to himself. She wanted to find him.

First she doused her light, and then she waited until she saw the elders flit about on their good-night rounds. The hollow tree began to darken as the fireflies fell asleep one by one.

There, she thought, when the last of the lights went out.

She turned and gathered her strength. This would be the first time she had ever ventured completely out of the woods alone. She was brave, but still.

"Firefly?"

Oh no. She turned in midair and tilted her head, trying to see who had caught her. *Fast fast fast, looooong looooong.* Phew.

"Yes, Elder?"

"What are you up to, out here alone?"

She hovered before him, her light still doused, and said nothing.

"Firefly? I asked you a question."

He floated back and forth, blinking in the slow, hypnotic pattern that the elders used to soothe the little fireflies to sleep. Despite herself, Firefly began to droop. She gave herself a shake to fight the tiredness.

"I'm going to look for a cricket," she admitted.

"Whatever for?"

"I like the way he sings."

"All crickets make music."

"Not like this one, though."

"How so?" said Elder, floating closer. "What makes this one different?"

"Well," said Firefly, suddenly unsure of herself. After all, the little cricket's song was a giant's song, and Elder was afraid of giants just like every other firefly. Still, she floated over to him and whispered in his ear. "He sings a song about baseball."

"Baseball? Baseball is a giant's game."

"I know," said Firefly, "but it's a really good song. And he's a really good singer."

Elder floated back and forth, still blinking in that hypnotic way. He hadn't said no yet, though, so she gathered up her courage.

"I'm just going to stay out a little longer," she said. "I won't go far."

She looked away from him so that she wouldn't be lulled into sleepiness.

"And it's so pretty out here," she added. "The stars. The moon."

She waited for him to start lecturing her, the way the other elders would have. After all, there were limits even to Elder's considerable patience. She waited for him to tell her that even though he admired the stars and the moon just like her, it was dangerous to spend too much time thinking about them. She waited, but Elder was silent.

"I'm not sure I can make you do anything, Firefly," he said.

"So I can go?"

"You can go, but before you do, look up at the sky with me for a minute."

They flipped onto their backs, and Elder traced the outlines of the constellations with one wing.

"That's the Milky Way," he said, "and that's Orion, and that's the Big Dipper."

Firefly followed his wing and nodded obediently. She was impatient to get going, but she stayed quiet.

"Pay attention now," Elder said. "You might need this information someday."

"I already know all about the constellations, Elder!"

"You don't know everything, Firefly. For instance, what would you do if you were far away from Firefly Hollow, and your wings were very tired, and you didn't think you could keep going?"

"That would never happen to me."

"But what if it did?"

"You'd come rescue me!"

"What if I was sound asleep and I didn't know you'd sneaked out?"

"Well, then, I'd . . . I'd just keep going."

"I'm glad to hear that. But there's another maneuver that might be useful in that circumstance. Let me show it to you."

Elder flew up to the top branch of the white pine.

"Watch," he said. "See what I do with my wings."

He let them float up above his head and then . . . he stopped fluttering them. His head drooping, Elder floated down, down, down. It was a mesmerizing sight.

"Your wings are like a parachute, Elder!" she shouted.

Just when he had built up enough speed that Firefly was beginning to worry, Elder lowered his wings and pulled up right in front of her.

"Exactly," he said, hovering. "That's why I call it

parachute formation. It will keep you aloft for a few minutes while you rest your wings."

"Can I learn it?"

"You can. Just make sure that you practice it far away from the other elders."

She blinked their secret code: *fast fast fast, looooong looooong*, which in this case meant *Of course.* Then she gathered her wings behind her and straightened up.

"May I go now?" she said.

He nodded, then floated backward and disappeared into the dark tree. With a mighty stroke of her wings, Firefly arrowed herself toward the river. Once out of the clearing, she found the animal path and stayed a few feet above it, pushing herself forward until she was fully out of the forest. Her wings were tired after a long night's flying, but she was determined.

Cricket music rose all around her. The closer she got to the river, the closer she listened. This was the farthest from the hollow tree that she'd ever been. She listened hard.

Over there!

The song was coming from the riverbank, just in front of a clump of tiger lilies.

Firefly took a deep breath, and with one final push of her tired wings, she swooped down and landed on the nodding stem of the tallest lily.

CHAPTER FIVE

PSST!

Cricket hopped slowly down the path to the riverbank as his classmates sang from the marsh and the woods and the cattails. The girls had set a lazy summer beat, just right for the boys to sing songs of sunlight and flowers and the smell of green grass. The same music that generation upon generation of crickets had sung.

Leap.

Leap.

Leap.

Now he was at the riverbank, where the rush of moving water covered up sound. Here Cricket could sing all he wanted, and no one would scold him. He perched in his usual spot by the tiger lilies, on the upthrust root of the white birch. Vole's boat was moored just beyond, but that was all right. Vole was no threat. He was a solitary creature who kept to himself and spent most of his time on his deck, practicing sailor knots. He didn't bother tiny creatures like crickets.

Before he began his song, Cricket looked back at Firefly Hollow. Most of his classmates didn't pay any attention to the fireflies, but sometimes Cricket liked to crouch at the edge of their clearing and watch a certain one practice her aerial maneuvers. He counted them off.

1. midair flip
2. loop-de-loop
3. figure eight

None of the other fireflies flew like this one did. He knew that the firefly elders forbade the young ones to fly farther than the clearing, just as Teacher forbade the young crickets to go anywhere near the giants' house, but this firefly, like Cricket, continually disobeyed.

What did it feel like, to fly through the air like that?

Cricket was a creature of the ground. He knew how it felt to spring high in the air—he excelled at High Jumping—but to fly? To soar through the air, to drift on the wind? It was almost beyond his imagination. The clearing was dark now, and so was the fireflies' hollow tree. They were asleep. Soon it would be time for Cricket to sleep too. The hours before dawn—neither fully dark nor fully light—were when the cricket and firefly nations rested.

He brought his wings together and sang softly.

"Take me out to the ball game
Take me out with the crowd.

Buy me some peanuts and Cracker Jack
I don't care if I never get back."

He tightened his grip on the root of the birch and looked out at the water, which was slow and quiet tonight.

If he practiced his baseball moves, would anyone see him?

He glanced around.

Cricket pictured Yogi Berra, the world's greatest catcher. He pictured Peter and his friend, how they used to play catch by the river. He pictured the baseball section at the Museum of Giant Artifacts. He leaped from the root of the white birch to the soft dirt of the riverbank, crouched down, and got a good grip with all six legs. Now he held his wings straight out, cupped them together, and imagined a baseball hurtling toward him.

Keep your eye on the ball.

Let it drop into your mitt.

Smack!

That *smack!* was the imaginary sound of the baseball thudding into Cricket's glove. Obviously he didn't have a glove—he was a cricket, not a giant—but if he did, that was the sound that the baseball would make. Oh, he could just hear it. He could just feel it. That white leather ball stitched with red. He half rose on four of his legs, reared his throwing wing back as far as it would go, and pretended to fling the ball back to the pitcher.

"Psst."

Yikes!

The sound was so startlingly close that Cricket nearly lost his balance and toppled backward onto his carapace. He hunched down and drew his wings together. All six legs were tensed, ready to leap if necessary.

The sound came again.

"Psst."

Cricket uncovered his head just enough to peer about. *Psst* was not a sound that crickets made. It was not a sound that Vole, just feet away on his boat, would make either.

Was it a giant?

He could hear Teacher's voice inside his head: *Giants are the greatest threat of all.*

Cricket drew in a deep breath. He told himself to be brave.

"Friend or foe?" he called to the darkness.

At first there was nothing. Cricket lowered his wings and looked in all directions. He sniffed the night air: pine woods and cold river water and cattails. Nothing strange. Nothing out of the ordinary. Maybe he had imagined the sound. From the boat, he heard Vole clear his throat.

"Friend or foe?" he called again into the night, just to make sure.

Then, from the darkness, a tiny glow appeared. It hovered in the air just above his head.

"Friend," said a small voice.

CHAPTER SIX

HOW BRAVE ARE YOU?

Firefly hovered over the little ground bug, blinking on and off.

Should she land next to him, on the riverbank, or should she stay in the air? This was the first time she had ever talked to anyone outside the firefly nation. She hadn't meant to scare him with that *Psst*, but his reaction was pretty funny.

"Friend?" he said now. "Are you sure?"

"I'm sure," said Firefly.

She floated down until she was suspended just in front of him. He peered up suspiciously. His wings—such as they were, those ground-bug wings that didn't really do anything—were half-raised, and his many legs were tensed.

"Who are you?" he said.

"I'm Firefly."

She hung in the air while he stared at her. His dark cricket eyes narrowed and turned even darker. A few feet down the shore, a creature coughed. *That must be the old river vole on his boat,* thought Firefly. She peered in the direction of the cough, but all she saw was a faint glow behind the tiger lilies. A lamp, maybe.

All the fireflies knew the story of Vole. How the river vole nation had been swept away in the Giant Flood, leaving only Vole, so little at the time, behind. How he had spent his life trying to teach himself the ways of his ancestors. But he must not have succeeded, because no one had ever seen Vole leave the safety of the riverbank.

Sad, thought Firefly. She tried to imagine being the only firefly in the world. She tried to imagine teaching herself to fly, without Elder hovering nearby, ready to catch her if she fell. It was a terrible thought.

The look in the ground bug's eyes was wary.

"What are you doing here?" he said.

"I came to find you."

"Me?"

"You."

"How do you know who I am?"

"You're the ball game cricket," she said. "Aren't you?"

Now the little ground bug's eyes widened. His wings and many legs seemed frozen in place. Were all ground bugs so tense? From the marsh and the woods and the fields, the other crickets sang their familiar summer music. Firefly twirled slowly, listening hard.

"All the rest of the ground bugs—" she began, but he interrupted her.

"Don't call us ground bugs. My name is Cricket."

"Cricket, then," said Firefly. "All the rest of the *crickets* sing about the river and the meadow and the trees."

He kept his eyes on her, that suspicious look back on his face.

"Cricket music is pretty," she added.

Ah. That relaxed him a little. One wing lowered itself.

"But you don't sing regular cricket music," she said. "You sing that giant song."

At that, he shot at least four inches into the air and landed with a thud, almost toppling onto his carapace.

"Do not!"

"Do so!"

"Do not!"

"Oh, stop it!" said Firefly. "Don't lie. We both know that the ball game song is a giant's song."

He started to deny it yet again, but she flapped both wings to stop him.

"If you're worried that I'm going to tell on you, I

won't," she said. "Fireflies are supposed to avoid the giants at all costs too."

She did a midair flip to emphasize her point.

"So what do you want?" he said.

"To tell you something."

"What?"

"That I like your song. It's not the kind of song that anyone else would sing."

He stared up at her with those dark eyes. Then, suddenly, he brightened.

"Hey!" he said. "I know you. You're the firefly who does the aerial maneuvers, aren't you?"

Yes! That was her! The ground bug knew who she was! All this time she had been listening for his song in the night, and he had been watching *her*? The thought made Firefly so happy that she spun in the air.

"Let me ask you something," he said. "How brave are you?"

"Very."

"Brave enough to come with me and see a giant up close?"

Firefly was so startled that she forgot to keep her wings moving and almost landed on the ground. A giant? Up close? But in the few seconds that it took her to hoist herself into the air again, she made up her mind.

"Show me the way," she said.

CHAPTER SEVEN

THE MINIATURE GIANT

Firefly floated along above the ground bug   oops, Cricket—and made up a new game called Zoom Out of Cricket's Way Each Time He Leaps. This game was harder than it looked. Crickets, or this one any-way, could leap much higher than she had thought.

Yikes! That was a close one.

"Are you trying to head-butt me?" she said.

"Maybe."

"Because it would be very easy for me to dive-bomb you. Did you ever think of that?"

No. Cricket hadn't thought of that. He imagined Firefly dropping from the sky onto his carapace like a tiny glowing bomb. It was a little too easy to imagine. Above him, Firefly smirked.

The sun began its gradual rise over the far pine woods. The air was still and calm and cool this early. The crickets were asleep, and so were the fireflies. Cricket was tired, but he liked knowing that he and this strange little firefly were the only two of their nations awake.

"Do you do this a lot?" said Firefly.

"Do I do what a lot?"

"Get up close to the giants."

"Well," said Cricket, "I've spied on the miniature giant lots of times. But I've never gotten really close before."

He tried to keep his voice nonchalant, as if being close to a giant was no big deal. But it was impossible. The elders had infected him with their fear after all. Just the sound of the word "giant" coming out of his own mouth caused Cricket to leap so high in the air that this time he really did head-butt Firefly.

"Ouch!"

Cricket rubbed his head with a wing and stopped short. Straight ahead lay the terrifying bulk of the giants' house. He couldn't seem to lift any one of his six legs.

Firefly hung in the air, blinking. "Um," she said. "Why exactly are we doing this?"

She pumped her wings just enough to stay aloft. She wasn't too eager to keep going either.

"I mean, the elders are always telling us that giants are the enemies of the firefly nation," she said.

"Same here," he said. "'Giants are to be feared. Giants are to be—'"

"'—avoided at all costs,'" she finished.

Cricket nodded. Any normal bug, ground or air,

would flee now while it still had a chance. He waited miserably on the ground, his wings closed tight to his sides. But Firefly didn't flee. She stayed, lifting her wings lightly.

"Why are we going there, then?" she said.

He looked up. She had said "we." That meant she wasn't backing out—she was going to come with him to the giants' house. He leaped straight up in the air out of happiness. Oh no. Another head-butt. This time the firefly was ready for him. She swooped down and dive-bombed him right on the carapace.

"Ouch," she said, rubbing the top of her head. "You ground bugs are harder than you look."

"So are you air bugs," he said. Firefly was tiny, but she packed a wallop.

They appraised each other admiringly. The sun was up now, and soft dawn light filled the air.

"Well?" she said.

"Well what?"

"Well, I'm still waiting for your answer."

"You really want to know?"

She nodded. The early morning sun glinted off her feathery wings.

"Because of the miniature giant," he said.

"The one they call Peter?"

Cricket nodded. "He plays baseball," he said, trying to explain. "I used to spy on him and his friend playing catch."

"I did too," admitted Firefly. "From the clearing."

She fluttered in the air next to a silver cobweb strung between limbs of a baby birch.

"For real?" he said. "Why?"

"Because," she said, "it looked like they were having so much fun."

She cleared her throat and began to sing.

"Take me out to the ball game
Take me out with the crowd."

Cricket joined in.

"Buy me some peanuts and Cracker Jack
We don't care if we never get back!"

"That's why I came to find you," she said. "You're the only other bug I know who's interested in anything to do with the giants."

"Giants invented baseball," said Cricket. "And I love baseball."

"Giants invented spaceships," said Firefly. "And I love outer space."

Cricket craned his neck and looked up at the sky, now a pale early morning blue. The moon was barely visible now, a ghost of its nighttime self.

"Why?"

"It's beautiful," she said. "The moon, and the stars, and the Milky Way."

She spun in the air, wrapping the silvery wisps of

cobweb around her like a blanket.

"Can you keep a secret?" she said. "Sometimes I dream about flying up there."

"But it's so far away!"

"I know it is. Do you think I'm crazy?"

Yes, Cricket was about to say. But then he thought about it. Firefly dreamed of flying to outer space, and he dreamed of being the first cricket Yogi Berra.

"No," he said at last. "I don't think you're crazy. I want to learn how to play catch. Do you think *I'm* crazy?"

She shook her head. Then the sun poked a finger of light onto the animal path, and Cricket sprang into action. They needed to keep moving. He leaped a little faster, and Firefly flew a little higher. Now they were at the shore, by the long, flat rock that Peter and his friend used to play on. The giants' house loomed before them at the bend of the river, so tall that it nearly blotted out the rising sun.

Cricket tried not to shudder. Above him, Firefly slowed to a hover.

"I'm kind of afraid to see a giant up close," she said. "If you want to know the truth."

"Me too," said Cricket.

Giants are to be feared.

Giants are to be avoided at all costs.

Giants are the enemies of the firefly and cricket nations.

Maybe this wasn't such a good idea after all. But then, before Cricket could turn around, the enormous front door of the enormous house burst open, and Peter the miniature giant came walking straight toward them.

CHAPTER EIGHT

COULD HE ACTUALLY SEE THEM?

Firefly and Cricket stayed where they were, hidden behind the long, flat rock. Cricket's wings half covered his head, and Firefly huddled just behind him.

Neither had ever been so close to a giant. They took turns peeking at him and then reported back in whispers, transfixed and terrified. The elders of both their nations always said that giants couldn't hear or see ground and air bugs, but neither wanted to take a chance.

"Is he by any chance holding a jar?" whispered Firefly.

Cricket lowered his wings and raised his head just enough to see.

"I don't think so," he said.

Firefly lifted herself up a few inches, until she could see both the miniature giant's hands. No jar.

"What's he doing now?" whispered Cricket.

"Just standing there," she said.

Maybe this was what giants did—just stand around—when they weren't crashing about inside their enormous houses or playing baseball. After all, they couldn't leap, nor could they fly. Firefly felt a tiny bit of pity for the miniature giant, huge though he was. Maybe Cricket felt the same way.

They watched in wonder as the miniature giant inclined his head first one way, then another. He appeared to be listening for something. But what?

Then, suddenly, he heaved a sigh.

Even hidden behind the rock, Cricket and Firefly felt the gale force of that sigh. Firefly was blown straight into an aerial backward somersault, and it was all Cricket could do not to flip over onto his carapace. Yikes!

Now the miniature giant turned and peered into the woods, in the direction of the clearing. He seemed to be looking for something. But what?

Another sigh! This time Cricket and Firefly were ready. But they weren't ready for what happened next. The miniature giant spoke.

"They must be asleep, I guess," was what he said.

What did *that* mean?

"Who's asleep?" said Firefly, forgetting to whisper.

"No idea," said Cricket, also forgetting to whisper.

The miniature giant whirled around.

"Oh no!" said Firefly.

"Duck!" said Cricket, and he scooted deeper beneath the overhang of the long rock.

Firefly didn't know if she should zoom straight up into the air or take shelter behind Cricket. There was no time to think, because with one step of his huge legs, the miniature giant was there.

Right there.

As in *right beside them.*

His enormous eyes looked back and forth, searching for something. Searching for . . . them? Firefly and Cricket held their breath.

"I was *sure* I heard something," said the miniature giant sadly after a moment.

Cricket and Firefly darted a glance at each other. Neither dared to say anything. A miniature giant was only inches from them. One more sigh and they could be blown halfway across the river.

Please don't be talking to us, thought Firefly.

Please don't be talking to us, thought Cricket.

Despite what the elders said—*they can't see you; they can't hear you*—it was terrifying to have those enormous eyes so close to them. The miniature giant stood up again—*whoosh!* Another gust of air—and trudged back to the far edge of the long, flat rock. "Everybody knows that crickets and fireflies don't talk, Peter," he said in a singsong voice.

"We do so talk," Firefly whispered to Cricket.

They huddled back behind the overhang, thankful to be alive. What would he do next? It was awful and fascinating at the same time. What he did next was spread his arms wide and open his mouth. They braced themselves for another blast of wind, but none came. Instead he began to sing.

> *"Take me out to the river*
> *Take me out to the sea.*
> *Build me a raft and a mast and a sail*
> *I don't care if I never get back."*

"Hey!" said Cricket, forgetting himself entirely. "Those aren't the words!"

Peter spun back. With one giant step he was back at their sides, crouching down by the overhang. *Now you've done it, you dumb ground bug,* thought Firefly, and she squinched her eyes shut. So did Cricket.

"Did I hear something?" said Peter.

"Nope," said Firefly. "You didn't."

"Shhh," said Cricket, and he poked her with one of his hind legs.

It was even scarier with their eyes closed. They felt him next to them, his hot giant breath. The seconds went by and Cricket, out of habit from Telling Temperature class, silently counted them.

One. Two. Three.

Four. Five. Six.

Firefly opened her eyes just a slit. The miniature giant was looking right at her! She darted a look at Cricket. His eyes were a tiny bit open too. He looked at her and then back at the miniature giant. *Flee,* thought Firefly. But it was too late to flee. *Play dead,* thought Firefly. But it was too late to play dead.

CHAPTER NINE

I KNEW YOU WERE OUT HERE

Peter sat back on his knees and nodded at Cricket and Firefly.

"I knew it," he said. "I *knew* I heard something!"

Cricket pressed his wings together. Firefly rose into the air a few inches and glowed once, then twice, before she could stop herself. She felt a *thud* coming on. She steadied herself and took a deep breath. *Be brave,* she told herself.

"Listen," she said. "Just tell us. Are you planning to kill us and eat us?"

"*What?*" Peter looked shocked.

Cricket took his wings off his head. "Yeah," he said. "Are you?"

"Kill you and eat you?" said Peter. "Why would I do that?"

"How should we know?" said Firefly. "That's the kind of thing that giants do, isn't it?"

Now it was Peter's turn to look scared.

"*Giants?* Where?"

"Right there!" said Cricket, and he pointed his wing at the giants' house. "You live with them!"

Peter looked at Cricket, then at the giants' house, then back at Cricket.

"I don't live with giants," he said. "I live with my mother and father."

"Exactly," said Cricket.

Peter looked even more confused. Firefly tried to clear things up.

"You *live* with giants," she said, "but you're not a giant. You're a *miniature* giant."

"No, I'm not. I'm a boy."

Cricket and Firefly weren't sure what to do at this point. It appeared that Peter didn't know he was a miniature giant.

"Well," said Cricket, trying to be diplomatic, "to us you're a giant."

"A *miniature* giant," added Firefly.

Peter looked at them thoughtfully.

"I guess I must look pretty big to you, huh?"

Pretty big? thought Firefly.

Try enormous, thought Cricket.

They nodded.

"The elders say that miniature giants are nothing but future giants," said Cricket.

"They also say that giants are the enemies of the cricket and firefly nations," said Firefly.

"And that . . ." Cricket paused.

"That what?"

"That you can't see us."

"Or hear us," added Firefly.

"That's crazy," said Peter. "I see you and hear you. We're talking right now, aren't we?"

He looked at Firefly and then pointed in the direction of the hollow tree.

"I've watched you fly."

"You have?"

"Yup. Every night."

He turned to Cricket. "And I've heard you."

"You have?"

"Yup. Down by the river, at night."

Cricket put his wings up over his head. All this time when he thought he was singing to himself, the miniature giant had been listening? The thought made him shy.

"I learned that baseball song from you," said Cricket, trying to explain. "Back when you used to play catch with the other miniature giant."

Now Peter sat all the way down on the rock and crossed his legs. He took a deep breath, and both Cricket and Firefly scooted under the overhang and braced themselves for dear life in case another sigh was coming. After a little while—no sigh—they emerged to find the miniature giant looking out at the river.

"But why did you change the words?" Cricket wanted to know. The ball game song was his favorite song. It was a perfect song, just the way it was.

"Because," said Peter.

"Because why?"

"Because my friend isn't here anymore."

"Why not?" said Firefly.

"Where did he go?" said Cricket.

But Peter didn't say anything else. Instead he stood up with a *whoosh* of air that almost slammed them both against the rock. Then he jumped off the rock onto the sand—another *whoosh*, but they were getting used to it now and knew to hold on tight—and ran back up the sand to his enormous house. Cricket and Firefly watched him go.

"Well," said Cricket, "we're still alive."

"Yes," agreed Firefly. "We are."

CHAPTER TEN

VOLE REMEMBERED EVERYTHING

F rom his boat, moored at the riverbank in the roots of the white birch and hidden behind the clump of nodding tiger lilies, Vole had watched the scene between Cricket and Firefly and Peter unfold.

Are you planning to kill us and eat us?

Kill you and eat you? Why would I do that?

How should we know? That's the kind of thing that giants do, isn't it?

Giants? Where?

Right there! You live with them!

The things these three didn't know about one another, Vole thought. The worlds of tiny creatures and humans were unbridgeable, or at least that's what crickets and fireflies were always told. But every once in a while a creature came along who questioned the elders. Every once in a while there was one—sometimes two—who ventured out of the firefly nation, out of the cricket nation, to test the waters on their own. Cricket was one of those creatures, and so was Firefly.

Vole had once been like that too.

Giants are the enemies of the river vole nation, his grandfather and the other elders had warned him when he was a young vole. *Giants are to be avoided at all costs.*

But, like Cricket, like Firefly, Vole had not listened. He had made friends with a boy, just like Cricket and Firefly were doing right now.

It was all so long ago, yet Vole remembered everything.

He folded his mended fishing net in a neat pile, laid it next to the rudder, and stood at the railing. Leaning out over the water, which sparkled under the soft early morning sun, he peered around the tiger lilies to see Cricket and Firefly huddled under the overhang of the long, flat rock. The boy stood tall above them and began to sing.

> *"Take me out to the river*
> *Take me out to the sea.*
> *Build me a raft and a mast and a sail*
> *I don't care if I never get back."*

What was this? Peter had changed the words to the song. Cricket and Firefly looked surprised as well. Vole leaned farther out over the railing and shaded his eyes with one paw. Peter ran off down the shore. Cricket and Firefly floated and leaped back down the animal path into the woods.

The river was fast today. There must have been a storm

far upstream, because something huge
was bobbing on the water, heading toward
Vole. Stormy days upriver always brought
giant artifacts. What sort of thing was
this? Ah, an enormous block of white. Vole
guessed it was a pillow, something that giants
used under their huge heads while they slept. But as it
came closer, he saw that it was a plastic milk jug, riding
high on the current.

"Build me a raft with a mast and a sail."

Vole made an instant decision and picked up his fishing pole. The silvery fishing line spun through the air at
just the right moment, and the hook plucked the plastic
milk jug up out of the water.

Then, with a single easy cast, Vole flung it through
the air so that the jug landed on the shore next to the big,
flat rock.

He would see what Peter did with it next time he came down to the shore.

The river water rushed by. It was always in a hurry, always in motion. All sorts of things ended up caught in it: sticks and leaves and dandelion fluff. Vole had seen many curiosities drift downstream from the giant houses that were built here and there along the river:

An empty crinkly bag that had once held giant food.

An enormous circle of ridged black rubber with a hole in the middle.

A glove, its four fingers and thumb puffed and hollow.

A baseball card, with the smiling face of a catcher, his mitt raised to catch an imaginary baseball.

And even a jar, a horrifying glass jar containing the bodies of dead fireflies.

Many of these giant artifacts were bigger than Vole's entire boat. Yet they went sailing past. Even the giants, big as they were, were no match for the power of the river. The river knew where it was going, and it went.

CHAPTER ELEVEN

THE FORK IN THE PATH

After Peter ran off, Cricket and Firefly set off for the Hollow. Neither said a word until they were well down the creature path. At the fork where Cricket turned left and Firefly continued straight, they paused.

"We just talked to a miniature giant, you know," said Cricket.

"I know," said Firefly.

"He wasn't that scary," said Cricket.

"He wasn't scary at all," said Firefly.

"Are you going to tell?"

"Are you crazy? No."

Cricket shook his head. "It'll be our secret," he said. "Shake on it?" He held up one of his legs, and Firefly brushed it with her wing.

"Shake," she said.

Then Cricket hopped left and she flew straight, and they both returned to their separate nations. Firefly balanced on the edge of her cubby, munching on a snail. She should be starving, but she wasn't. It was quiet and peaceful inside the hollow tree at this time of day. The spiderweb hammocks swayed in the cubbies, each holding a young firefly.

Elder appeared before her, an inquiring look in his eyes.

"Well?" he whispered. "Did you find the cricket?"

"Yup."

"And?"

"And what?"

"Was he singing the baseball song you like so much?"

"He was."

"Did you talk to him?"

"I did."

Elder smiled. "About what?"

Firefly leaned forward so that no one else in the tree could possibly hear.

"He told me that he dreams about learning how to catch," she whispered. "And I told him that I dream about flying up to the moon."

She left out the part about the miniature giant. She couldn't tell anyone, not even Elder, about that. Ever. *It'll be our secret,* Cricket had said, and they had shaken on it.

"So you have a friend now," said Elder.

"I already have a friend. You."

"But now you can talk to Cricket. You can tell him your secrets."

"He's a *cricket*," said Firefly.

"Still. I might not always be around."

"What do you mean?"

"What I mean," Elder said, "is that I'm getting old. Very old."

"You are not!"

But even as she said the words, Firefly knew they weren't true. Elder hovered in front of her cubby. His wings were nearly transparent, and his blinks were lighter and lighter with every passing night. She shivered. She didn't want Elder to get any older.

"Firefly."

He waited until she looked up and met his eyes.

"Did you know that when fireflies get very old, they turn into stars?"

"*What?*"

Could this be true? She pictured the night sky in her mind. All those thousands of glimmering stars, so high above. Was it possible that every star was a firefly from the past? If so, how had they gotten up there? Elder was nodding.

"It's true," he said.

"But—"

"And what that means," he continued, "is that if the day ever comes when I'm not here, I'll be up in the sky."

"But—"

He raised a wing to stop her protest.

"Just remember that," he said. "Remember that one of the stars in the sky will be me, and I'll be watching over you."

Then he blinked their secret code: *Fast fast fast, looooong looooong*. She forced herself to blink back. There was so much she wanted to ask him about, but talking would mean acknowledging the idea of Elder not being there, and that was something she couldn't bear to think about. So she stayed silent, and Elder floated off on his rounds of the other cubbies. Finally Firefly fell asleep. She slept long and hard, and as she slept she dreamed of falling stars.

That night, when the moon was fat and yellow in the sky, the fireflies woke up and streamed out of the hollow tree into the cool night air. The babies worked on Basics of Blinking—signal straight, signal left, signal right— while Firefly and her friends practiced more advanced techniques. Most were still trying to master elementary maneuvers—hovering with minimal wing motion, tight spirals around the circumference of the white pine—but Firefly had moved far beyond them. Tonight she drifted to the very edge of the clearing and practiced parachute formation alone, the way Elder had told her to.

She worked especially hard tonight. Parachute formation was a difficult maneuver: wings up high, head drooped, legs dangling, letting the breeze waft her back and forth but always down. Down and down and down. It was a strange and unusual maneuver, but she was getting better at it.

Practice makes perfect, thought Firefly.

Forgetting Elder's warning to practice this particular

maneuver far from the others, she buzzed up to the first big branch of the white pine and drifted down in parachute formation, into the midst of the young fireflies.

"That's creepy, Firefly," said one of her friends.

"Yeah," said another. "You look dead when you do that."

"It gives me the willies," said another.

Gee, thanks, thought Firefly. None of the others were interested in aerial maneuvers. They stuck to the basics. She said nothing, just zoomed straight up and practiced parachute formation again.

When she was done, she flipped onto her back. There was the moon, glimmering so high in the sky. How long would it take to fly up there? Would it be possible to do it in a single night? If she left for just a few hours and then came zooming back home, would anyone even notice she was gone?

CHAPTER TWELVE

IF I COULD

E ven though Cricket hadn't told anyone about meeting the miniature giant, Teacher sensed something. Cricket was whispering in the corner with Gloria—telling her about meeting Firefly, how she'd nearly scared him to death when she first appeared—when Teacher rapped on her desk to get his attention.

"Excuse me, Cricket. Do you have something to share with the class?"

Cricket did have something to share with the class; in fact, he had lots of things to share with the class, but one mention of any of them and Teacher would stick him straight in detention.

"We're waiting, Cricket."

Gloria poked him in the leg with her good wing. "Tell her something," she whispered.

"Um," said Cricket. "Telling the temperature is one of the main purposes of a cricket's life?"

Teacher sat back and clicked her wings once. Twice. Again. "It is," she said. "It certainly is. But is that the important thing you were discussing with Gloria?"

Gloria poked him again, a poke that meant *Say yes.*

"Yes," Cricket began, but Teacher cut him off.

"I don't believe you, Cricket. That's strike one. Three strikes and you're out. Isn't that the rule?"

Yikes! *Three strikes and you're out?* That was baseball language.

"That's right," said Teacher, as if she could read his

mind. "It's been clear for some time that you've got an unhealthy fixation on giants. But baseball, Cricket? Baseball? After what your friend"—she pointed to Gloria—"went through with a *lollipop stick?*"

She shook her head and went on. "A lollipop stick weighs a fraction of what a baseball weighs. You are on very dangerous ground here, Cricket."

The other young crickets leaned forward. One of them, out of Teacher's sight line, sat back on his hind legs and raised a wing in the air and pantomimed the motion of a baseball catcher. The others around him started to laugh, muffling their mouths with their wings.

So they knew.

They all knew about Cricket's fascination with baseball. And they all thought that he, Cricket, was a joke. Cricket folded his wings and looked down at the dirt floor.

"Back to Telling Temperature," said Teacher. "You're next, Cricket."

Cricket shook his head. He had no idea where they were. What did it matter, anyway, what the temperature was?

"Well?" said Teacher. "Three chirps in fifteen seconds plus thirty-seven equals what temperature?"

"I don't get it, Teacher," said Cricket. "I don't see the point."

He didn't. All you had to do was hop outside to know how warm or cool it was. And anyway, if all the other crickets knew what the temperature was, why did they need him to do the exact same thing? Learning to catch would be so much more useful to the cricket nation. If crickets knew how to catch, never again would one of them be injured by a falling object like a lollipop stick. Right?

Teacher cleared her throat loudly.

"Strike two, Cricket," she said.

Just then, far off in the distance, gleams of light shivered through the clouds. Distracted, Teacher leaped to the window and motioned the class over with one wing. Cricket stayed back. From the other side of the room rose the sound of whispered counts, all beginning with *One*, and all beginning at different times. *One, two, three—one, one, two, three, three, four, one.* The whispers were drowned out by the booming thunder.

"Ch-ch-ch," came a whisper from behind him.

It was Gloria, trying to get his attention. Gloria, with her draggy legs and wing. Gloria, who couldn't jump, who usually faded into the background of the class, literally faded, every day pushing herself against the far dirt wall so that Teacher wouldn't use her as an example in Fear of Giants. He turned.

"I hate this, Cricket. Don't you?"

"You know I do."

"Who cares about the temperature?"

"Not me."

Her strange blue-green eyes were bright and burning. She poked him with her wing again, more like a jab.

"Why don't you do something about it, then?" she whispered.

Cricket looked around the room. Young crickets labored with their pencils, muttering numbers to themselves. Faraway lightning flashed in the faraway clouds beyond the windows. Teacher roamed up and down the orderly row of young crickets at the window, checking calculations. She hadn't yet noticed that Cricket and Gloria were conferring again.

"Like what?" he said.

"Leave."

Gloria waved her good wing at the other crickets crouched with their notebooks and pencils. Beyond the window, beyond the grass and the path that led to the river, was the river itself.

"Escape," said Gloria.

She waved her wing again.

"Don't just sneak out for a few hours," she said. "Escape."

Again came the sparkle from the distant water, followed by another *boom* of far-off thunder. The young crickets crouching by the window busily scratched away in their notebooks, counting under their breath.

"I just want to learn how to catch things," said Cricket.

Gloria blinked slowly, her blue-green eyes disappearing and then reappearing. She was crying. Far off in the distance, the river glinted. The storm was over. The young crickets closed their notebooks and started to return to their desks.

"I'd go with you if I could," whispered Gloria. "But I can't. Leave, for both of us."

Teacher turned and saw them.

"Back to your seats," she said. "Both of you. And since you appear to be so smart that you don't need to pay attention like the others, I want to hear your temperature calculations. Now."

Cricket turned to go back to his desk, but then he stopped. He just . . . stopped.

"What seems to be the problem, Cricket?" said Teacher.

"Nothing."

She nodded briskly, once, as if he had confirmed something.

"Strike three," she said. "You're out. Detention for the rest of the week."

She clapped her legs together, in a hurry-up-get-moving way. Cricket moved faster. He was almost at his desk now, the desk where his notebook lay unopened, his pencil beside it. The other crickets looked at him with a what's-he-done-now look. Here he was at the desk.

Cricket reached out with one of his front legs as if to pull his chair out and sit down, but then he surprised himself and swept the notebook and pencil off. *CRASH.* The other crickets jumped. Behind him, he heard Teacher suck in her breath. He leaped once, into the aisle. He leaped again.

And he kept on going, right out of the school.

CHAPTER THIRTEEN

WOULDN'T IT BE AMAZING?

Late that night, when the baby fireflies had already gone to bed and the older ones, Firefly's age, were nearly done with flying practice, Firefly flipped onto her back.

"What are you looking at, Firefly?" said one of the others.

"The same thing she's always looking at," said another.

"Not the moon again."

"Always with the moon."

"You should look at it," said Firefly. "*Really* look at it. Wouldn't it be amazing to fly up that high?"

Uh-oh. She had said too much. The other fireflies buzzed and vibrated and blinked frantically, the way they always did when Firefly said something that startled them. At least no one had thudded to the ground. Yet.

An elder, an old and extremely stern elder, came to see what all the clicking and vibrating was about. Seeing Firefly, she scowled.

"What's going on here?" she said.

"She's talking about flying to the moon," blurted one of the young fireflies.

"Fireflies don't fly to the moon. Put that idea out of your mind at once."

The hollow tree began to come to life as other elders within stirred. They came darting out of the knotholes, one after another, and formed ranks behind the first elder. The young fireflies buzzed and fluttered until the whole clearing glowed bright.

"The giants flew to the moon," said Firefly. "And they don't even have wings."

Thud. Thud. Thud.

Young fireflies fell to earth all around her. While others attended to them, the old, stern elder floated over to Firefly. She glowed with a furious light.

She waited until Firefly met her gaze.

"The only possible outcome of an attempt to fly to the moon," she said, "is failure. Giants are the enemies of the firefly nation."

"All of them?" said Firefly. "Are you sure? Because the miniature giant seemed so nice when Cricket and I were talking to him. His name is Peter."

Cricket? Peter? Giants? The moon?

Now she'd truly done it. Not to mention she'd just broken her promise to Cricket. She glanced away from the stern elder's horrified eyes to see the others staring at her. Something had changed, just now, and they all felt it. In talking with a giant, she had disobeyed the cardinal rule of the firefly nation. She needed Elder, and quickly. He would understand. He would explain to the others.

"Where's Elder?" she said.

"We're here," said one of the others, speaking out from the long line of ranked elders.

"Not you," she said, forgetting to be polite. "Where's *my* elder?"

The elders floated silently before her. Some of them blinked private messages to one another, none of them in Firefly and Elder's secret code. She twirled around, blinking the *fast fast fast, looooong looooong* code. *He must be out there somewhere,* she thought, and again she blinked out the code. And again. But there was no answering blink, not from nearby, and not from far off.

"Elder!" she called.

Then the stern old one cleared her throat.

"He's gone," she said.

"What do you mean he's gone? Out foraging? Flying?"

But she just shook her head. "Gone," she said again, and pointed to the sky.

Elder, gone?

Firefly followed the pointing wing. Thousands of stars winked and glimmered in the darkness. No. Elder could not be gone. Not when she needed him so badly. The stern elder's glance softened when she saw the look on Firefly's face.

"I'm sorry, Firefly," she said. Her voice, for such a stern elder, was gentle. "It was time."

"No, it wasn't!" she said. She darted back and forth in the clearing. "Elder!" she called. "Elder!"

No answer. No welcome sight of Elder emerging from the hollow tree. The air in the clearing buzzed and vibrated.

"Elder!" she cried again, but the knothole in the hollow

tree remained dark. She glanced wildly around but saw only the blinking of little fireflies and the sad gaze of the remaining elders.

That was when Firefly zoomed straight up, aimed herself at the giants' house, and left the Hollow behind.

CHAPTER FOURTEEN

WHY DID YOU LEAVE?

*S*troke.

   Stroke.

   Stroke.

Firefly counted out her wingstrokes to calm herself, the way Elder had taught her. Now Elder, *her* Elder, was gone. He had turned into a star. This was what became of all fireflies, he'd said, but she wasn't ready. There were things she needed to tell him, things that only he would understand.

Remember that one of the stars in the sky will be me, he had told her. *And I'll be watching over you.*

That wasn't enough! She needed to talk to him. She needed to tell him about Cricket and Peter and the giants and the moon. She flipped onto her back and searched the sky. It was full of stars, but which one was Elder? She flipped back and kept on flying, the night air cool against her fevered body.

When she was close to the giants' house, Firefly slowed. She steadied herself in midair and then pulled herself straight up with light wing strokes. Now she hovered outside Peter's bedroom. His window was open. Firefly floated closer and closer, until she was just outside the screen.

Breathe.

Breathe.

Breathe.

That was his calm, even breathing. She peeked in. She could just make him out, curled under a white sheet on a huge bed. One arm and one leg were thrown outside the sheet, as if he had fallen asleep in the middle of doing something. One foot rested on the bare wooden floor. Firefly hung in the air outside his window, watching him sleep. She began to sing softly to herself.

"Take me out to the ball game
Take me out with the crowd."

By morning she herself was half-asleep, keeping herself aloft with a few lazy strokes of her wings.

"What are you doing?" said a familiar voice.

Cricket! Where had he come from? Crickets were supposed to be in cricket school this time of day.

"Are you spying?" he said. "Because if you're spying, I want to spy too."

With a mighty leap he made it to the window ledge and managed to hang on with all six legs. It was a precarious perch. Firefly hovered just above him.

"Why aren't you in class, Cricket?"

"Why aren't *you* with the rest of the fireflies?"

"Because."

"Because why?"

Firefly didn't want to talk about Elder. Not yet.

"Because I told them about the giants and the moon and you," she said.

"What?! Why did you do that? I thought we had a deal."

She did a backflip in the air above his head. "I couldn't help it," she said. "I'm not good at keeping secrets. So I left."

"Well," he said. "I left too."

"Why did *you* leave?"

"Because they were laughing at me. And Teacher was angry and put me in detention because of the whole baseball thing. And, well, because I was failing Telling Temperature class."

"Well," said Firefly, "I'm failing Fear of Giants class."

"You are?"

"Yeah. I told the fireflies that I wanted to be like the giants and fly straight up to the moon."

"You didn't."

"I did."

He shook his head. "What did they do?"

"They forgot how to fly," she whispered. "Thud. Thud, thud, thud."

Cricket started laughing and nearly fell off the perch. He renewed his grip with all six legs.

"Hey!" said Firefly, peeking again into Peter's room. "He's awake!"

Together they watched Peter fling back the sheet and hop out of bed. He stretched and yawned and pulled on his T-shirt and shorts. He thumped across the wooden boards of the floor and disappeared. Now he was visible behind the next window, the kitchen screen window. Firefly floated over, and Cricket, with another mighty leap, landed on the kitchen window frame.

Oh no. The mother and father giants were up too.

How enormous they were. So much bigger than Peter, and so clumsy. Look at the father giant, roaming around inside the kitchen with a telephone in one hand and an enormous orange bowl in the other. Look at the mother giant, sitting in that enormous chair with a giant green mug on the table before her.

"Beth, have you seen my—?" said the father giant.

"No, but have you checked in the—?"

"Yes. Not there."

What did that mean? How confusing. Cricket and Firefly couldn't stop watching, though. Three giants, right in front of them! Peter sat down at the table, and the father giant put a plate in front of him. He picked up a fork and began to eat. *Clink. Scrape.*

"That smells horrible," Firefly whispered to Cricket.

"How can he eat it?" whispered Cricket.

They felt sorry for poor Peter, forced to eat that awful-smelling giant food. *If only he had a snail,* thought

Firefly. *If only he had a nicely rotted piece of tomato,* thought Cricket. But Peter kept clinking and scraping. The stinky food didn't seem to bother him.

The father giant kissed the mother giant on the cheek and ruffled his hand on Peter's head. *If he did that to me, I'd be dead,* thought Cricket, and for a minute he imagined the lollipop stick as it must have looked, roaring toward Gloria on that awful day.

"Bye, honey," said the father giant. "Good luck with that project."

"Thanks," said the mother giant. "Drive safe."

The door of the giants' house burst open, and the father giant tromped down the path to his car, opened the door, and leaped in. *Slam.* Cricket felt that slam vibrate from the bottom of his six legs up through his carapace and all the way to the ends of his wings.

Grind.

Roar.

The sound of the car starting was familiar to both of

them, but neither had ever been this close to it before, and it was louder than either could have imagined. The father giant couldn't seem to do anything quietly. Now the tires crunched down the gravel driveway and eased onto the smooth road, and the car disappeared around the bend.

"Bye, father giant," whispered Firefly, and Cricket, despite himself, started to laugh. Peter turned his head sharply in their direction.

"Uh-oh," whispered Cricket. "Now you did it, Firefly."

At that, Peter's eyes widened, and he pushed back his chair. *Tromp, tromp, tromp.* He appeared at the window and pressed his nose to the screen.

"Cricket! Firefly!" said Peter. "Are you spying?"

"Um," said Cricket. "Kind of."

"Peter?" called the mother giant. "Who are you talking to?"

"Cricket and Firefly. Do you want to meet them?"

Tromp. Tromp. Tromp.

The mother giant lumbered across the kitchen floor and peered down from her enormous height. Cricket froze on the window frame. Firefly momentarily forgot to fly and almost thudded to the ground.

"The ones you were telling us about last night?" she said.

The hot gust of her breath through the screen, even from so high above them, washed over Firefly and Cricket like a wind.

"Oh yes," said the mother giant. "There they are. Cute."

Firefly uncovered her eyes just enough to see that the mother giant wasn't really looking at them.

"She's just pretending," whispered Firefly to Cricket. "She doesn't really think we're his friends."

She zigzagged through the air like a firefly doing an obstacle course, but the mother giant just smiled vaguely and turned away.

"I'm going to get to work, sweet boy," she said. "Stay

where I can see you through the window. What are you up to today?"

Peter shrugged. The mother giant put her hands on his shoulders and rested her chin on the top of his head.

"Listen," she said. "Do you want to talk about Charlie?"

"Nope."

The mother giant sighed. The force of her sigh through the window screen blew Firefly back in the air a few inches. Cricket held on to his perch for dear life, all six legs gripping the wooden frame. These giants. They didn't know their own strength.

CHAPTER FIFTEEN

LET'S NOT GO BACK

It was a long day for Cricket and Firefly, a long day without sleep, without school, without the usual routines of the cricket and firefly nations. They weren't quite sure what to do with themselves. They spent most of the day spying on Peter from the safety of the clump of tiger lilies at the base of the white birch. Neither of them wanted to risk getting as close as they had the day before. After all, he *was* a giant, even if he was miniature.

First he skipped stones on the river.

Then he made a sand castle.

Then he dragged driftwood into a big pile.

Then he sat cross-legged and looked out at the water for a long time.

No leaping. No flying. No one to play Death by Giants with. Well, on second thought, maybe that wouldn't be a game Peter would choose to play.

"Kind of boring," Cricket whispered to Firefly.

"*Really* boring," said Firefly.

Finally the sun began to sink, and cricket music began to rise over the field and at the edge of the marsh. Peter headed back to his house. Deep in the clearing, the other fireflies began to emerge from the hollow tree. Cricket and Firefly dreaded the return to their nations.

"If I go back now," said Cricket, "Teacher would just lock me up for good."

"I'm pretty sure the fireflies don't want *me* back

either," said Firefly. "They think I'm nuts." She paused, then said, "Can I tell you something?"

"Yeah."

"Elder turned into a star."

"*Your* elder?"

"Yeah."

They were quiet for a minute.

"He was the only one—the *only* one—who didn't think I was crazy," said Firefly. "He was the only one who would look up at the moon and the stars with me."

"I'm sorry," Cricket said. "I'm really sorry, Firefly."

"Thank you."

He brushed her wing with his front leg. It felt so much like Elder, the way he used to brush her wing with his, that Firefly started to cry.

"All I know," she said, wiping the tears from her eyes with one wing, "is that I can't go back there."

"I guess I can't go back either. Not unless I want to spend the rest of my life in detention. What will we do, though?"

"Stay here. Spy on the giants some more. The big ones."

"But the big ones are scary," said Cricket.

She hovered in front of him. The sun had slipped all the way below the far side of the river now, and she began to glow.

"We're just spying," said Firefly. "We're not risking our lives. Come on."

Cricket gave in. The sounds of giant dinner drifted out the kitchen window.

Swoop!

Leap!

"Have some more peas, Peter," said the mother giant.

"I don't like peas."

"Have some anyway," said the father giant. "They'll help you grow big and strong."

What a strange thing to say. Why would giants want to be any bigger or stronger?

Clink. Chomp. Gulp.

The sound of giants eating was not pretty.

"We should start thinking about school, Peter," said the mother giant.

"No, we shouldn't," said Peter.

The father giant cleared his throat.

"Peter," he said. "Your mom told me what happened this morning, and—"

"If you're going to tell me I should talk about Charlie, stop!"

Firefly zoomed straight up in the air so that she could see inside the window. Peter sat perfectly still, looking down at his fork. Each tine held three speared peas.

"Besides," Peter said, "I did talk about him already. With Cricket and Firefly."

The mother and father giants looked at each other above Peter's head.

"You talked about Charlie with your imaginary friends?" said the father giant.

"They're not imaginary. And don't make fun of me."

"Oh, Peter," said the mother giant. "We're not making fun of you. Your dad used to have an imaginary friend too."

Firefly hovered outside the window screen, watching. The father giant leaned back in his chair, frowning at the mother giant.

"I did?"

"According to your mother, you did."

"What sort of imaginary friend?"

"Some kind of rodent," said the mother giant. "She told me that you used to spend all day, every day with him, one summer. She gave up trying to talk you out of pretending he was real."

"That's funny," said the father giant. "I don't remember anything like that."

But he leaned back in his chair and stared up at the ceiling, as if he was trying to remember something that he had forgotten. Firefly watched, so intent that she scraped against the screen.

She needs to be careful, thought Cricket. *If they look out the window, they'll see her.*

But Firefly was heedless, so focused was she on the father giant and the strange expression on his face. So was Peter. Then the father giant quickly shook his head and brought his chair back down with a thump. *Yowch.* These giants were just so . . . giant.

No one said anything after that. They concentrated on their plates of hot, horrible-smelling giant food, and when he was finished, Peter pushed back his chair and ran down the hall to his room. The mother and father giant looked at each other.

"What are we going to do?" said the father giant. "I'm more and more worried."

"He misses Charlie," said the mother giant. "Don't push him."

"He needs a friend, Beth. An *actual* friend, not imaginary friends."

At that, Firefly looked down at Cricket. Imaginary?

How infuriating. She flew straight at the window screen and shouted in.

"Hey!" she shouted. "He's got me and Cricket!"

She dive-bombed the screen, regardless of the dangers of concussion.

"We're not imaginary!" she yelled, and she dove again.

The mother giant and father giant looked up at the window.

"What *is* that?" said the mother giant.

"Some kind of bug, brushing up against the screen," said the father giant. "A moth, maybe."

A moth? What creature in its right mind would mistake Firefly for a moth? Moths bumbled through the air, throwing themselves at lightbulbs and frequently frying themselves in the process. Moths were heavy-winged and . . . and . . . drab! Being compared to a moth made Firefly even more furious.

Swoop!

Back at the screen she flew. She dive-bombed it again and again, smashing her head against the wire mesh.

"That's no moth," said the father giant. "I think it's a firefly."

"Fireflies don't act like that, David."

Bang!

Bang!

Bang!

"This one does," said the father giant. "It must be insane."

Insane?

Bang!

Bang!

Bang!

"You're the insane ones!" yelled Firefly. "We're not imaginary! We're ACTUAL!"

"That is definitely a firefly," said the father giant. "A firefly run amok."

"Well, I don't want it in here," said the mother giant. "Let's close the window."

The father giant rose from the giant table and tromped over to the window.

BANG.

Cricket and Firefly looked at each other again. Enough was enough. Without saying a word, they turned and *Leap! Swoosh!* back to the riverbank they went. Firefly turned to Cricket.

"I'm actual."

"So am I," said Cricket.

"We're actual!" shouted Firefly. "Take that, giants!"

She swooped up and around a young maple tree to emphasize her point.

"What does 'actual' mean?" said Cricket, once she had returned.

"It means . . . it means . . . hmm," said Firefly.

She fluttered in the air, blinking on and off. It was a quiet night, and the moon hung low in the dark sky.

"Actual means . . . ," said Firefly, trying again.

But she didn't know what it meant, and neither did Cricket. Then, from a few yards away, behind the tall tiger lilies, they heard someone clear his throat.

"Real," said an unfamiliar voice. "Actual means real."

CHAPTER SIXTEEN

THE PAPER BOAT

Vole set down his rope—he was practicing a sheet bend tonight, a knot that was used to tie two lines together, according to the *River Vole's Guide*, and it was a difficult knot to master—and headed for the bow of the boat. Firefly was darting back and forth in the air, while Cricket did little hops along the sand.

Vole cleared his throat and said it again.

"Real. Actual means real."

Silence. Had he scared them both voiceless? Firefly hung in the air, nearly motionless, while Cricket froze on the sand below like a bug statue.

"Who said that?" whispered Firefly.

"I think it was the vole," Cricket whispered back. "The one that lives on the boat."

"Hello," called Vole. "I can hear you."

Silence again. Vole almost laughed.

"Should we go down there?" whispered Firefly.

"Maybe," whispered Cricket. "Teacher and the elders say he's not dangerous."

"I can still hear you," called Vole.

Silence again. How long had it been since Vole had said anything to anyone but himself? A long time.

"He can still hear us," whispered Firefly.

"I know," whispered Cricket. "That's what he just said."

"Should we go?"

"We might as well."

The little bugs approached with great caution. Moonlight gleamed on the polished brass railing, and Firefly floated along just above its curved length.

"Your elders are right," said Vole. "I'm not going to hurt you."

The little bugs regarded him in silence. Then Cricket eyed the distance, made one great leap, and perched on a coil of rope.

The boat creaked pleasantly as the current tugged it out to the length of the mooring rope and then nudged it back to shore again. Out, and back. Out, and back. The boat had been built to last many a generation of river vole, and Vole took excellent care of it. Firefly did a little spiral dance around the mast, and then she darted through the open door that led from the deck into Vole's cozy living room and back out again.

"We're actual, you know," she said to Vole, hovering in front of him.

"I know you are," said Vole.

"The giants told Peter we're not real," said Cricket.

"I know they did."

"But why?" said Firefly.

"They can't hear us, that's why."

"So it's true then?" said Cricket. "The elders are right about that?"

"They are."

"How do you know, though?" said Firefly.

Cricket perched on the coil of rope, his wings folded close to his sides the way they always were when he was thinking hard about something.

"I know," said Vole, and something in his voice made her be quiet.

Firefly zoomed straight up in frustration and then spiraled around and around until she was dizzy. *Swoop!* Down she floated, through the dark night air, back through the living room door, down and down until she came to rest on . . .

. . . a boat.

A paper boat, set in the middle of Vole's polished wooden table.

This was an old boat. Firefly could tell from the stiff, parched feel of the paper from which it was made. She reached out one wing, very gently, and touched it. She was afraid that paper this old might disintegrate, even at the light touch of a firefly's wing, but it held steady.

Cricket hopped up onto the table and crouched next to the boat. He, too, reached out a wing to touch it.

"Whose boat is this?" said Firefly.

"Mine," said Vole.

"It's old," said Cricket.

"Really old," said Firefly.

"It is," said Vole, and he put a furry paw lightly on the prow of the old boat.

As far as Cricket and Firefly knew, Vole lived alone and he fished alone. There were reports that he could be glimpsed fishing off the deck of the boat, and he was often seen tying intricate knots in a length of rope. His fur was a rich brown and he usually wore a fisherman's cap pulled low over his brow. There was no Fear of Vole class, nor did the elders ever caution the youth of the firefly and cricket nations against Vole.

But the sad story of how he came to be the only surviving member of the proud river vole nation was sometimes told late on warm summer nights. And whenever the story was told, the young crickets and fireflies shuddered in sympathy. They could not help him, though, since none of them knew the secrets of sailing.

Vole was getting older, thought Firefly. Maybe he would never leave the riverbank. She shivered. She did not want to be like Vole, stuck forever at the edge of the Hollow. She floated in the air next to the ancient paper boat.

"Where did you get this boat?" said Firefly.

"Someone gave it to me," said Vole.

"Who?" said Cricket.

"A giant."

What? This was so surprising that Firefly nearly thudded straight down, but she managed to recover before she hit the table. Cricket leaped straight into the air.

"You were friends with a giant?" said Cricket.

"A miniature giant."

"Then you *do* know that the elders are wrong," said Firefly. "Miniature giants do see us, and they do hear us."

Vole said nothing.

"Right?" said Firefly.

He still didn't answer. Firefly, with her sharp firefly eyes, was able, even in the dim moonlight from the deck, to see that there were words written on the boat. She skimmed her wing over them.

"What does this say?"

"I don't know," said Vole. "It's written in giant language."

The three of them—Cricket and Vole and Firefly—examined the mysterious words. What did they say? Who were they meant for?

Cricket yawned. Firefly's head drooped and then bobbed back up as she caught herself from drifting down, out of the air. It was late. They were so tired. But after what had happened that morning, how could either of them go back to their nations?

Cricket rested against the old paper boat and half closed his eyes. Firefly spotted a spiderweb in the corner and floated over to it. It was a raggedy sort of web, but it still looked so inviting. Wouldn't it feel good to lie down and be rocked to sleep in that spiderweb? She drifted closer and closer. Whatever spider had made it was long gone.

"Mr. Vole?" she said, trying to be as polite as possible.

"Yes, Miss Firefly?"

"May Cricket and I stay here?"

Cricket's eyes snapped open. Stay here? With the river vole? On the boat?

"Here? On my boat?" Vole sounded surprised.

Firefly nodded.

"But won't your elders be looking for you?"

"Teacher is angry at me," said Cricket.

"And Elder," said Firefly, "my Elder, I mean, well . . ." Her voice trailed off.

Vole looked at her closely. Was she crying? He thought of his grandfather, and for a moment he heard the old vole's voice in his mind. *You'll know when the time is right.* Vole made an instant decision.

"Yes," he said. "You're both welcome to stay here."

"Thank you," said Firefly, and she let herself float down into the soft strands of the spiderweb.

"Thank you," said Cricket, and he let his eyes close fully.

Vole sat in his chair by the fire and watched the little creatures sleep. Cricket coughed. Firefly's spiderweb swung gently with the rocking of the boat in the current. It was so strange to have anyone besides himself on the boat. And when was the last time either Cricket or Firefly had eaten? When they woke up, they'd be hungry. If he peeled some carrots and cut them into tiny pieces, would they eat them? Vole went to work in the galley.

When Firefly woke, Vole brought her an acorn shell filled with tiny pieces of carrots—not the food of a firefly, but she tried them anyway. Not too bad. Nothing like a delicious snail, of course, but really not bad. Cricket snapped his down immediately.

"My head hurts," said Firefly.

"That's what happens when you dive-bomb a giant's house," said Cricket. *True,* thought Firefly. But it had been worth it.

She tipped herself out of the raggedy spiderweb hammock into the air and fluttered about the living room of the boat.

"We're *actual*," she said.

Despite her aching head she did a midair flip, and then another.

"Actual!" she called. "Actual!"

CHAPTER SEVENTEEN

LET'S BUILD A RAFT

N ext morning Peter came out of the house with his hands full of artifacts. Firefly and Cricket stared from the safety of the clump of tiger lilies. Any one of the things he was carrying would be worth an entire exhibit in the museum.

A blue blanket with tiny stars all over it.
A red balloon tied to a stick.

A ball of twine.

"Cricket!" he called. "Firefly! Are you out here?"

Peter was calling them! They raced each other down the shore to where he was waiting by the long rock over-hang, the artifacts clutched to his chest.

"Guess what?" he said. "We're going to build a raft."

Just then, from inside the giants' house, came the earthshaking *tromp tromp tromp* of the mother giant's footsteps.

"Peter?"

The mother giant stood calling from the kitchen window, one hand pressed against the screen.

"Yeah, Mom?"

"Who are you talking to?"

"Cricket and Firefly."

"Oh," she said. "Right."

Tromp. Tromp. Tromp. She walked across the kitchen floor toward the front door. The entire house vibrated slightly with each footfall. *Tromp. Tromp. Tromp.* Now she was on the porch. Now she was there, on the sand, right in front of them. If Cricket took one small leap, and Firefly drifted just a few inches forward, they could touch her. Yikes.

The mother giant touched the blanket in Peter's arms.

"What are these things for?" she said.

"We're going to build a raft."

"And what's the raft for?"

Peter didn't say anything.

"Honey? What's the raft for?"

"I don't want to tell you."

"Why not?"

"Because," said Peter, his voice small. "It's none of your business."

"Peter!"

The mother giant bent down so that she was the same height as Peter.

"What did you just say?"

She put her enormous hand under his chin and tilted his head up so that he was looking straight at her.

"Do you hear me?"

Peter didn't say anything.

"Listen to me. I know you're sad, but you still can't talk to me like that."

"No, you don't," said Peter.

"No, I don't what?"

"Know how sad I am."

The mother giant inhaled a long, long breath. "She's going to blow," Firefly whispered to Cricket, and they both prepared for another tornadic gust of wind. But instead, the mother giant put her arms around Peter and hugged him.

The mother giant kept her arms around Peter for a long, long time. Neither of them said anything. Finally, the mother giant sat back on the sand and held Peter's hands in hers.

"You're right," she said. "I don't know how sad you are. But I'm your mom and I'm here and I'm watching out for you."

I'm watching out for you, thought Firefly. Those were like the words that Elder had said to her—*I'll be watching over you*—and hearing them made her miss him fiercely. She looked up at the sky, but it was daylight. No stars were visible. Was he really up there somewhere?

The mother giant stood up.

"I'm going to be in the kitchen," she said to Peter, "finishing that project for my client. Stay where I can see you through the window, okay?"

Peter nodded, and she bent down and kissed the top of his head. After the mother giant went back into the house, Peter stooped and pulled an empty plastic milk jug out from underneath the rock overhang.

"Look at this!" he said. "I found it yesterday—a perfect flotation device for the raft."

He gathered driftwood from the shore and knotted it

together with the twine, piece by piece. His knots were careful and firm.

"Why are you making a raft?" said Cricket.

"So I can make a quick getaway if I need to."

"Why would you need to make a quick getaway?" said Firefly.

"Well," said Peter. "My mom and dad keep talking about school, and I don't want to go back to school."

"Why not?"

"Because Charlie won't be there."

He picked up a stone from the shore and hurled it into the river, where—*plunk*—it sank immediately.

"We used to wait for the bus together," he said.

He picked up another stone, and another, and another, and one by one he threw them into the river.

"And I'm not going back to school without him," he said. "No matter what they say."

"Good for you," said Firefly. "The giants don't know everything."

"They're not giants," said Peter. "They're my mom and dad."

"Your mom and dad don't know everything, then," said Firefly.

It felt weird not saying "giants," but if Peter wanted her to say "mom and dad," she would try.

"That's right," said Cricket. "Moms and dads aren't always right."

"What about yours?" said Peter suddenly. "What are your parents like?"

Firefly parents? What a funny idea.

"We don't live with parents," said Firefly. "Fireflies all live together. In a hollow tree."

"Crickets all live together too," said Cricket.

Peter looked at them, one to the other, as if he was trying to figure this out.

"No parents?" he said.

They shook their heads. A strange look passed over Peter's face.

"But who tucks you in at night?" he said. "Who makes you breakfast in the morning? Who helps you with your schoolwork?"

"The elders," said Firefly.

She thought about Elder, *her* Elder. For a minute she wanted to tell Peter about Elder, how he had swooped underneath her and saved her life when she was a baby firefly, how he had taught her parachute formation, how they'd had their own secret code. But she didn't.

"We don't have school," she said instead. "The elders teach us to fly, and once we know how, we're free. Sort of, anyway."

"Sort of?"

"We're supposed to stay in the clearing," she said.

"Why?"

"Well. Because of all the dangers out here."

"What kind of dangers?"

Firefly wasn't sure what to say. Peter stood looking

at her, with his head tilted, waiting. Should she tell him the truth?

"Um, giants," she said. She didn't want to hurt his feelings, but it was the truth. "We're supposed to stay away from giants."

"Why did you leave, then?"

"Because I want to fly up to the moon."

"And they don't like that?"

"Nope. The elders say I'll fall right out of the sky."

All but one elder, she thought. Peter looked up at the sky. It was a long way up there.

"That wouldn't be good," he said.

"It wouldn't," agreed Firefly. "But if you giants can do it, then I can too. Right?"

"But we have spaceships."

"And I have wings."

It was true, Firefly did have wings. Peter turned to Cricket.

"What about you? Do crickets have school?"

"Yes," said Cricket. "I'm supposed to be there right now."

He pictured the School for Young Crickets. They were probably in Fear of Giants class at this very minute. Teacher was probably standing in front of the classroom, describing, for the billionth time, the day that the lollipop stick had come flying out of a clear blue sky and broken Gloria's leg and wing. The little crickets were probably listening openmouthed, the way they always did. He could just imagine Teacher's voice, the way it lowered as she got to the end of her story: *And that, crickets, is why you should always avoid giants.*

"Why aren't you, then?" said Peter.

"Because," said Cricket, and he shrugged a wing.

"Because they all laugh at him," said Firefly.

"Why?"

"Because he wants to be a baseball player," she said. "Excuse me, a baseball *catcher.*"

Oh no. Cricket closed his eyes. He waited for Peter

to start laughing at him, just like all the crickets did. A cricket, wanting to be like Yogi Berra. It was ridiculous, when you thought about it. Who did he think he was? He waited for a giant gust of laughter to blow him backward onto his carapace, but no gust came.

He opened his eyes a slit and looked at Peter, who was smiling.

"I could teach you to play catch," he said. "If you want."

CHAPTER EIGHTEEN

YOU DID IT!

The very next day they began Cricket's How to Catch a Flying Object lessons. Peter marked off a distance of three yards on the sand with two pieces of driftwood. Firefly practiced straight-line flying between them until Cricket told her to stop because she was distracting him. He perched on top of one piece of driftwood, and Peter stood behind the other.

"You're pretty small," said Peter.

"You're pretty big," said Cricket.

"*Pretty* big?" said Firefly. "He's a giant!"

Then she saw the look on Peter's face. "Miniature giant, I mean."

"Okay, Cricket," said Peter. "What kind of flying objects do you want to begin with?"

"Baseballs!" said Cricket.

"Are you nuts?" said Firefly. "A baseball would kill you!"

"She might be right," said Peter. "Let's start with something a little smaller."

He began by tossing Cricket little stones, but that didn't work out so well.

He then tried tiny pebbles, but that didn't work out either.

Then he tried maple seeds, but even when he crouched a few inches away from Cricket and tossed them as lightly as he possibly could, Cricket ended up flat on his carapace. His legs waved feebly in the air until Peter flicked him upright again.

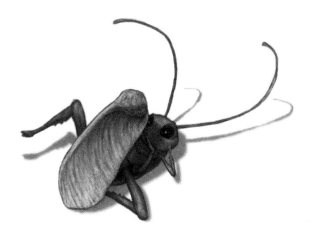

"Wow," said Cricket. "Catching a flying object is a lot harder than it looks."

He held his front legs out and flexed his feet. He was an agile creature, able to leap nearly a foot in the air. But when it came to catch, his strong legs weren't much use. Neither were his wings. They made music, and they helped him keep his balance, but when he tried to clap them together around a seed, what he ended up with was air.

"What about dandelion fluff?" suggested Firefly, looking at the tiny white fluffs drifting down to the sand on the gentle breeze. Some landed on the surface of the water, where they floated for a while before the river swallowed them up.

Peter looked dubious. Dandelion fluff was light, but so were maple seeds, and Cricket hadn't been able to catch them. Still, it was worth a try.

Cricket leaned back. The first fluff that floated his way veered left at the last moment, and his wings clapped together on nothing.

"Pay attention!" yelled Firefly.

Cricket focused. Peter crouched next to them and watched.

"Incoming!" yelled Firefly.

A fluff came drifting down from the sky, straight toward Cricket's upraised wings. He leaned back, wings held perfectly steady. Oops—the fluff twisted on the breeze and changed course. Cricket leaned a little to the left. Oops—another change of direction. Cricket leaned a little to the right. Wings up and outstretched, legs tensed and ready, forward a bit more, now backward, and—

"You did it!" shrieked Firefly.

She somersaulted backward in surprise. Cricket held his wings above his head and hardly dared to breathe. Had he actually caught the fluff? Slowly he brought his wings down before him and opened them.

Peter sat back on the sand and smiled.

"You did it," he said. "You really did."

Cricket looked at the dandelion fluff, trapped between his wings. He placed it on the sand. There it was, white and light. And he, Cricket, had managed to catch it as it drifted down. He looked up at Firefly, still somersaulting, and Peter, still smiling.

"I can't believe it," he said. "I caught something."

"First, dandelion fluff," said Peter, "and next, who knows?"

"This day will go down in history," said Firefly. "This is a day for the Museum of Giant Artifacts!"

"What's the Museum of Giant Artifacts?" said Peter.

"Um," said Firefly, "it's a . . . museum."

"A museum that's supposed to be a *secret*," said Cricket, giving Firefly a look. "Forget she said anything."

"Too late for that," said Peter. "What's in this museum?"

"Giant things."

"Like what?"

"Scary things," said Firefly. "Things like the Jar."

"The Jar?"

Peter waited for her to explain. But how could she explain the awfulness of the Jar to him?

"You wouldn't understand," she said. "Giants like to catch fireflies and put them in jars to die."

"But you keep calling *me* a giant, and I don't do that."

"You're a *miniature* giant. And you're not like the others."

Peter looked troubled.

"Just so you know," he said, "I've never put a firefly in a jar."

Cricket decided to change the subject.

"The museum has other things in it," he said. "There's a baseball. A baseball glove. And a picture of Yogi Berra, the world's greatest catcher."

"Is that where you got the idea of being a catcher?" said Peter.

"Yeah. Partly."

"And watching you and your friend was the other part," said Firefly. "He used to spy on you."

"On me and Charlie?" said Peter.

"Yup," said Firefly. "He used to sneak down here and spy on you two playing catch on the beach. That's where he learned the song."

"What song?"

"This one," said Firefly, and she sang. *"Take me out to the ball game. Take me out with the crowd. Buy me some peanuts and Cracker Jack—"*

But Peter was shaking his head, motioning for her to stop.

"Don't sing that," he said.

"Why not?"

"Because."

"But it's the song you and the other miniature giant used to sing," said Firefly.

"I already told you to stop calling him a miniature giant!" said Peter. "His *name* is *Charlie*."

He jumped up from his crouch—the ground shook beneath Cricket, who held on to the shifting sand beneath him with all six legs—and ran down the shore—*thump, thump, thump*—to the big rock, where the half-finished raft was stored. He stood on it, looking out at the river.

"He's not going to leave, is he?" said Firefly.

"I don't know," said Cricket.

"I don't want him to leave."

"Me either."

"What's he doing?"

"I think," said Cricket, "that he's missing his friend."

Cricket thought hard, and he made a decision. He

gathered his legs beneath him and leaped down the sand to Peter.

"I'm sorry about Charlie," he said.

Peter said nothing. Cricket forged on anyway.

"Do you miss him a lot?"

"He was my best friend."

Cricket thought about this. It would be terrible to miss a best friend. He remembered all the times he had spied on Peter and Charlie, playing by the river.

"I know I'm just a cricket," he said. "And Firefly is just a firefly. But if you want, we can be your friends."

Peter didn't turn his head—he was still looking out at the river—but he took a deep breath. Cricket braced himself for a gust of wind, but nothing happened. Then Peter turned and nodded.

"Okay," he said.

CHAPTER NINETEEN

SHE JUST WANTED
TO KEEP GOING

The next morning Cricket stretched his wings and all six legs and leaped off Vole's table onto the floor.

"Let's go see if Peter's up," he said.

"Race you to the raft!" said Firefly, and they took off.

They were well matched. Each had a special strength: Cricket could leap nearly a foot in the air, and Firefly could arrow herself straight ahead.

Cricket won, but just barely. Meanwhile, Firefly got up so much speed that she soared right past the big rock where the raft was stored and straight out over the river. She let herself be carried on an updraft, glancing down at the trees and water and boat receding below. Was this what flying up to the moon would feel like?

She just wanted to keep going.

Cricket shaded his eyes with a wing and watched Firefly, soaring high above the river. Was she ever going to turn around? What did it feel like, to be blown around in the sky like that? Maybe it felt the same as when he gathered his legs beneath him and then *sproing! sproing! sproing!* leaped along the ground.

He watched as Firefly kept going, higher and higher, and for a minute he was filled with a terrible fear that she was never going to come back.

Then, at the last minute, just as he was losing sight of her so high up, she pivoted in the air and came swooping back down.

"Did you see me up there?" she asked, out of breath. "Can you believe how high I was?"

Then she rested in the air just above Cricket to wait for Peter. They didn't have to wait long. There he was, his hands full of more giant artifacts: a yellow rubber duck with a painted-on smile and a big plastic bubble from a packing box. He pulled the raft out from under the rock.

"Another flotation device," he said, poking the big plastic bubble with a piece of driftwood.

SLAM.

The father giant emerged from the front door of the giants' house. He stretched his giant arms and lifted his face to the sunny morning sky. Then he looked down the shore where Cricket bounced up and down on the big plastic bubble and Firefly did loop-de-loops above him while Peter tied more driftwood together.

Oh no! The father giant wasn't heading their way, was he?

This was the time of day when he got into his car and

turned on the engine and crunched and roared his way down the road and disappeared around the bend. This was when the mother giant usually leaned out the front door and called to Peter that she was going to be working on her computer in the kitchen, or on a conference call, and to stay where she could see him from the kitchen window.

But that didn't happen today.

Instead the father giant put down his bag and came walking straight toward them. Cricket jumped off the big plastic bubble onto the neck of the yellow rubber duck, clasping it with all six legs. Firefly joined him, hovering just behind the duck's rump, shivering in fear. But the father giant didn't seem to notice them.

"Hey there, little guy," he said, and he crouched down on the sand next to Peter.

"Hey, Dad."

"What are you up to this morning?"

"Just working on my raft with Cricket and Firefly."

The father giant smiled. He reached out and rubbed Peter's head. He didn't seem to hear the part about Cricket and Firefly, which was a relief to both of them. They stayed as motionless as they could, hiding behind the bright yellow duck.

"They're right here," added the boy.

Again the father giant didn't seem to hear. Cricket and Firefly snuck a look at each other, a look that meant, *Do giants not even hear their own miniature giants?*

"Peter, school starts in three weeks."

The boy didn't say anything. He tied some driftwood together. The ball of twine was shrinking.

"And we need to get some things straightened out," the father giant said.

He picked up a stick and dragged it through the sand. Then he reached out and rubbed Peter's head again.

"Are you scared to go back to school without Charlie?"

"Nope."

"You sure?"

"Yup."

"Why not?"

"Because I'm not going back to school."

"Hang on," Cricket whispered to Firefly, "the father giant's going to sigh." Cricket was right. The gust of wind swept over them, but they were ready. The father giant opened his mouth to speak, then closed it, then opened it again. He chose his words with care.

"What are you going to do instead?"

"Stay here. Teach Cricket to play catch. Keep track of Firefly's endurance flying."

"Your imaginary friends?"

"They're not imaginary! They're actual."

Firefly turned to Cricket.

"See?" she whispered. "We're actual."

"Watch out," whispered Cricket. "The giant's going to sigh again." He flattened himself against the ducky's neck, and Firefly huddled closer to its behind. The father giant shook his head, stood up, and brushed off his pants.

"Okay then, kiddo," he said. "We'll figure this out later. I'm off. Another day, another dollar."

"Dad. They're actual. They're right here."

But the father giant was already walking away.

CHAPTER TWENTY

EVERYTHING GOES SOMEWHERE

They spent the day working, Peter on the raft, Firefly on her upward zooms and endurance laps, and Cricket on fluff catching.

An empty plastic peanut butter jar sailed by, and Peter snagged it with a stick and bound it underneath a corner of the raft. Cricket, next to him on the sand, crouched low. Every time a piece of dandelion fluff drifted by on the wind, he leaped up and clapped it between his wings.

"Let it come to you," he whispered to himself, repeating what Peter told him during Catch a Flying Object lessons. "Wait for it."

Firefly, meanwhile, did forty-two endurance laps as a warm-up and then began zooming straight up and then straight back down again. Over and over she practiced her upward zooms. It wasn't easy, because fireflies were drifters by nature. But she was getting better and better at it.

She eyed the river, sparkling next to the three of them. She remembered the feel of the wind when she raced Cricket to the shore, and how it swept her up and carried her out to the middle of the river. She remembered how it felt to fly higher and higher, to leave Firefly Hollow behind.

She snuck a glance behind her.

Cricket was oblivious, jumping up and down, chanting baseball phrases to himself: "Keep your eye on the ball! Let it come to you! Can of corn! I got it!"

Firefly snuck a glance to her right. Peter was intent on the task of binding the rubber ducky to a piece of driftwood.

Firefly snuck a glance straight up, into the blue sky. A single puffy white cloud floated above the river. It didn't look that high.

"Yes!" That was Cricket, another dandelion fluff clutched between his wings. The puffy little cloud was farther than she'd ever flown before. But it would be good practice for the day she flew all the way up to the top of the sky. Should she? *Could* she?

Only one way to find out.

Swoop!

With a single powerful stroke of her wings, Firefly zoomed up. She lifted her wings and pushed them down, down, as hard as she could.

Swoop!

She fought the pull of gravity and kept going. It took all her powers of concentration to rise straight up like this.

She was probably close to the cloud by now. Better check. She tilted her head back for a second.

Hmm. That cloud really didn't look any closer.

Now she looked down. Far below, Cricket was making frantic little leaps back and forth on the sand. Peter was waving with both arms. Now he cupped his hands around his mouth and shouted something. Firefly couldn't even hear what he was shouting, she was so far up. Aha! So she *had* made progress.

Show them what you're made of, Firefly, she told herself, and she gathered her strength for another mighty stroke.

Whew. All this gravity fighting had tired her out. She looked down again. Now Peter circled both arms in the air, a motion that meant, *Come back.* Cricket leaped from the raft to the sand and back again.

They were worried, that was obvious. And she was tired. Very tired.

"Okay, boys," she called, although neither could hear her. "Incoming!"

She lifted her wings high, let her head droop, and aimed herself toward the shore in parachute formation. This was so much easier than trying to fly against the pull of gravity. Down and down she fell, finally pulling herself up a few feet above Peter's head.

"What do you think you were doing!" yelled Cricket.

"You scared us," Peter added.

"If I'm going to fly up to the moon," said Firefly, "I've got to start somewhere, right? Like with that cloud."

She flipped on her back and pointed up with her wing—but the cloud was gone. What? It was there just a minute ago. Had it disappeared? Oh . . . there it was. Way downstream, floating high above the river. This fly-to-the-moon business might be more complicated than she'd thought. But she kept that to herself.

"Why do you want to fly up there so much?" said Peter. "I'm serious."

What a dumb question, thought Firefly. "Wouldn't

you want to?" she said, pitying him for those heavy arms of his and his lack of wings. "If you could?"

He shook his head. She stared at him and then turned to Cricket. He shook his head too, but he was staring at the puffy little cloud far downstream now. He had tilted back on four legs and half raised one wing. Was Cricket pretending that her cloud was a baseball? Yes. He was. She felt a little sorry for him. She felt sorry for them both. Peter was still looking at her.

"Well, *I* do," she said. "I want to fly up to the moon. Even if no one else in the firefly nation wants to, I do."

"And I want to learn to catch," said Cricket. "Even if no one else in the cricket nation wants to, I do."

"And even if everyone else wants me to go back to school," said Peter, "I'm not going."

He looked down the river. Firefly's tiny cloud had vanished.

"That means that we're our own nation," said Peter. "We're the nation of Peter and Cricket and Firefly."

★ ★ ★

It was late afternoon now. The sun, that big orange ball, was low in the sky. The mother giant had finished her work for the day and closed her computer. Now she tromped about inside the kitchen, clattering those noisy pots and pans. Firefly and Cricket and Peter stowed the raft safely for the night under the big overhanging rock. The father giant came roaring back in his car. Soon it would be dinnertime, and the mother and father giants would call Peter to come eat. Peter stood up and stretched. Then he looked at Cricket and Firefly.

"Where do you go when you die?" he asked.

They stared at him. What a strange question.

"What do you mean?" said Cricket. "Crickets don't go anywhere."

"Everything goes somewhere," said Peter.

"Not crickets. We stay right here. We turn into music."

"You can't sing when you're dead."

"That's not what I mean."

Peter tilted his head in the way that meant he was trying to figure something out. How could Cricket explain to him?

"After we die, we *turn into* music," he said. "And we're everywhere." They turned into the sound of the wind, rustling the leaves on the trees.

The crunch of an acorn in the fall.

The *tap-tap-tap* of a woodpecker's beak on a tree.

All these sounds were music. Crickets and the memory of them were still part of the world, even if they were invisible.

"We're everywhere," Cricket said again, but he could tell that the boy didn't really understand.

Peter turned to Firefly.

"What about fireflies?"

Firefly spread her wings wide.

"Elder told me that when we get very old, we turn into stars," she said. "So we're still here too, I guess. Up there."

The three of them looked up at the darkening sky, just beginning to glimmer with the light of the fireflies of the past.

"What about people, then?" said Peter. "Where do we go when we die?"

This was a question that neither Cricket nor Firefly had ever thought about before. Cricket shook his head.

"I'm sorry, Peter," he said. "I don't know."

"Me either," said Firefly.

Peter stood there on the sand, waiting for more. But they had no idea what to tell him.

CHAPTER TWENTY-ONE

SOMETHING NEW

The days were shorter now. The sun rose on the far side of the pines later every morning, and it sank below the far side of the river earlier. The leaves of the big maple tree by the giants' house were not quite as green as they had been, and they looked a little tired.

Peter and Cricket and Firefly spent their days on the shore, each of them busy both separately and together.

"Cricket!" Firefly would yell. "Time me!"

She waited until Cricket was ready, then took off from a hovering position. Vertically if it was a day for upward zoom practice, horizontally for endurance laps. In either case Cricket, with his superior sense of counting, was her timer. He was getting tired of it, though. The stronger Firefly got, the longer he had to count. It reminded him a little too much of Telling Temperature class.

Cricket, meanwhile, worked and worked on his catching technique. Peter patiently watched as fluff after fluff drifted down from the sky and Cricket reared back or leaped forward, wings extended.

"Not bad," he would call. "A little more extension on your right wing and you've got it," or, "Good try. Let it come to you next time."

And Peter worked on the raft. Day by day he made it more seaworthy, tying and retying flotation devices, adding more driftwood, letting the entire raft out on a rope a few feet into the river to check for watertightness and then hauling it back in.

Every night the fireflies gathered in the clearing, lighting the Hollow with their glow. And every night the crickets filled the forest with music as Firefly and Cricket made their way to Vole's boat. He was always there, waiting with leaves full of chopped carrots and cattail tubers, wild dandelion greens and morsels of fried fish.

When they were full, they sat next to Vole in the living room while he mended his fishing nets or practiced his sailor knots. Sometimes he showed them the knots, his paws carefully twisting and tying the worn lengths of rope into intricate patterns. He explained what each knot was used for—to tie two lines together, to secure an anchor, to attach a line to an object.

"When in doubt, use a bowline," said Vole. "That's what my grandfather always told me."

"Why?" said Cricket.

"I have no idea," said Vole. "But that's what he said. He told me that a sailor has to know all the sailing knots."

"But you're not a sailor," said Firefly. "Are you?"

"Not yet," said Vole. "But I am the last living river vole. And all the river voles who came before me were sailors."

It was hard for Cricket and Firefly to imagine Vole anywhere but here, on his boat moored to the white birch. This was where he had been as long as they could remember.

"Vole?" said Firefly.

"Yes?"

"Does this mean that you want to sail away from Firefly Hollow?"

"Someday," said Vole. "Someday."

Firefly and Cricket were silent. Neither of them wanted to think about a day when Vole would not be here. They watched his paws moving swiftly on the rope. And when they couldn't keep their eyes open any longer, Firefly hoisted herself into the spiderweb hammock and Cricket leaped to the table and lay down next to the ancient paper boat.

The darkness of the forest was darker now, and the crickets' voices sounded fainter than they had in June, when the light was long and the air soft and tender. When Firefly and Cricket woke in the morning, they were grateful for the fire that Vole lit now in the fireplace.

"It's still summer, you know," said Firefly to Cricket.

"Yes," said Cricket. "It's still summer."

"It *is*," insisted Firefly, who could hear the lack of assurance in his voice.

"And our practice is paying off," said Cricket. "You're getting better at high altitude and endurance laps, and I'm getting better at catching. I'm about to move up to oak seeds, you know. I'm going to try, anyway."

"I know," said Firefly.

What were she and Cricket going to do, though, once they'd mastered the arts of flying and catching? They had left their nations behind. When Firefly finally flew up to the moon, there would be no fireflies to admire her. When Cricket finally mastered the art of catching falling objects, none of the other crickets would know.

"Do you think we'll all stay together when summer's over?" she said. "You and Peter and me, the nation of three?"

Cricket stretched his wings in the pale early morning sunlight on the deck. He thought about it.

"What else would we do?" he said. "Where would we go?"

"I don't know," said Firefly.

Now was the time when other little creatures began to think about warm places to sleep the winter away. Some of the other little crickets even eyed the giants' house, which was always warm. This was the time of year that the elders stepped up their warnings. Cricket could just imagine the scene taking place nightly in the cricket nation and at the School for Young Crickets. He had lived through it before.

"If you enter their giant homes," the elders would drone, "they will hunt you down and sweep you out the door with their giant brooms."

Their dark eyes glared around the circle of listening young crickets.

"And that's if you're lucky," they hissed.

Cricket used to imagine what a giant broom would feel like, crashing down on his carapace and flinging him out a giant door.

"They cannot bear the sound of our music," the elders said. "They call it 'chirping.'"

"You don't want to know what the giants are capable of when they're in a mood," they said.

But Cricket now knew they were wrong. He and Firefly had spent the summer with a giant—a miniature giant—and no harm had come to them.

After warming up by the fire and eating the breakfast Vole had made for them, Cricket and Firefly headed for the giants' house. Cricket crouched on the kitchen window frame, while Firefly hovered just above the window-sill. Peter was eating his cereal—*clink, clink, clink*—and the mother and father giants drank their dark, steaming liquid out of their giant mugs. The mother giant tapped her fingers on the edge of her mug.

"So," she said, leaning forward. "School starts in two weeks."

Peter said nothing.

"We know it won't be the same without Charlie," said the father giant.

"But there are lots of other kids there," said the mother giant. "And guess what?"

Clink. Clink. Clink. Peter kept eating his cereal. The mother and father giant waited, but he didn't say anything.

"There's a new family moving in down the road," said the mother giant.

"Yeah," said the father giant. "A new family!"

Clink. Clink. Clink.

"Aren't you a little bit excited?" said the mother giant.

"Nope."

Clink. Clink. Clink.

"I already have friends."

The mother and father giants looked at each other above Peter's bent head.

"They're imaginary friends, Peter," said the father giant.

"They're not imaginary. They're actual."

Firefly turned to Cricket and gave him a *See? We're actual* look. Then she spied some unfamiliar things in the corner of the giants' kitchen.

"Hold on," she said. "What's that over there, Cricket?"

Cricket gathered his strength and—

Sproing!

—up from his perch on the window frame he leaped. He clung to the wire mesh of the kitchen window screen and peered in. Everything looked the same as it always did.

Tall wooden counters. Yellow-painted cupboards. The enormous circle of *tick, tick, tick* on the wall. The wooden table with four chairs and woven place mats. The pitcher filled with hydrangeas and wild roses and tiger lilies. The fireplace, its dark unlit hearth holding a grate filled with pieces of wood.

"Over there," Firefly said, pointing with one of her spindly legs. "See?"

There, in the corner next to the fireplace. There, in a small pile set neatly on a chair with a caned seat.

A blue pack with straps. A box of narrow yellow sticks. A box of thicker colored sticks. A small pair of the same tool the mother giant used to cut flowers. A packet of white paper. Even from this distance, Cricket could see that the paper was lined. What did it remind him of?

"Hey," he said. "Does that paper remind you of something?"

She pressed herself further against the screen and squinted.

"Nope," she said after a moment. "Nothing."

"Something on Vole's boat."

"Quit being so mysterious and just tell me."

"The paper boat," whispered Cricket. "Vole's paper boat."

Vole's paper boat? This time she thought a little longer. The packet of lined paper, white and rectangular, seemed to glow from where it sat among the other supplies on the caned chair.

"You're right," she said.

The two little creatures hung outside the window screen, gazing in at the pile of shining white paper. They pictured Vole, quiet Vole, mending his fishing net in his lap at night, its silvery filaments spilling onto the deck below. They pictured the ancient paper boat, set in the middle of the polished wooden table, glowing in the lamplight of Vole's living room.

CHAPTER TWENTY-TWO

WATCH ME!

Hey!" yelled Firefly. "Watch me!"

She balanced on the rubber duck's rump and then zoomed straight up into the cloudless blue. She flew so fast that everything around her—the white birch, the river below, Peter and Cricket looking up—blurred together. When she ran out of steam, she slowed to a hover and looked down.

"Well?" she called down to Cricket. "How fast?"

"Three seconds!"

Three seconds. Her best yet. All this practice was paying off. Soon she would definitely be able to get to the moon and back in a single day. *Take that, giants,* she thought. They had their silver spaceships, but she had wings.

"Now watch *me*," said Cricket when she floated back down to the raft.

He crouched on the very edge, just above the lashed-on plastic milk jug.

"Are you watching?" he said, and he pointed to a leaf fluttering down from the maple tree. "I'm going to try a maple leaf!"

Firefly said nothing. There was no way he would be able to catch something so big. Yes, he'd come a long way from the beginning of the summer. But this was not a fluff; it was a leaf. It was at least twice as long as Cricket's body.

"Are you watching?" yelled Cricket, and he waved both wings in the air.

"Watching," said Firefly.

"Watching," said Peter.

Cricket sprang off the edge of the raft, wings open, and—

—oh no—

"Yikes!" said Firefly.

She hovered as Peter pulled the leaf off Cricket. He lay dazed on the sand, flat on his carapace.

"Did I catch it?" he said.

"Well . . . ," said Firefly.

"Kind of," said Peter.

He reached down and flipped Cricket upright and helped him up to the raft. Compared to Peter, the raft was tiny. Compared to Cricket and Firefly, the raft was huge.

"Peter!" came the call from the giants' house. "Dinnnnnnnner!"

Peter pushed the raft under the rock and turned to Cricket and Firefly.

"Tomorrow morning?" he said.

"Tomorrow morning," said Firefly and Cricket.

Firefly zoomed high into the air above Peter's head.

"Race you," she said.

"Me too!" said Cricket.

And they were off, the three of them, to see who could get to the giants' house first. So far, Cricket or Firefly had always won.

But tonight was different. Tonight Peter covered three times as much ground in a single stride as one of Cricket's leaps. Cricket tripled his efforts, but it took all his strength to keep up the pace. Firefly pumped her wings as hard as she could, but even she could barely keep up. By the time Peter jumped onto the first step of his porch, the tiny creatures had just managed to stay even.

"I almost won!" said Peter. "I almost beat you!"

Cricket and Firefly were too out of breath to do more than pant. Cricket flopped on his carapace on the stone in front of the giants' porch. Firefly fluttered her wings just enough to stay afloat on the air. The mother giant suddenly appeared right behind the window screen.

"PETER! DINNNNNNER!"

Cricket clapped his wings over his ears. Firefly spiraled over and over, bowled over by the sheer force of giant decibels. Just as she recovered, and just as Cricket gingerly removed one wing from one ear, came another giant shock wave.

"I'M RIGHT HERE!"

Was that *Peter*? Neither of them had ever heard him make such a loud sound.

"Well, come on in, then," said the mother giant.

And in went Peter. *Slam.* The sound of the front door closing behind him was louder than either Cricket or Firefly remembered it being. *Scrape.* Even his chair, as he pulled it out from the table to sit down, was louder than they remembered.

"Did you hear that?" said Cricket, once they were safely on their spying perch.

His voice was full of surprise.

"Of course I did," said Firefly. "It was hard to miss."

"Peter was as loud as the giants."

"I know."

They looked at each other then, but said nothing. They didn't have to. Each knew what the other was thinking. The voices of the elders sounded in both their heads: *Miniature giants are nothing but future giants.*

Later, when Peter was asleep, they spied on the mother and father giants at the kitchen table.

"I don't know what to do," said the father giant.

"Me either," said the mother giant.

"I don't know how to help him," said the father giant.

Firefly floated up a few more inches, so she could get a better view. The mother giant was looking down at the table.

"He won't talk about him," said the father giant.

"He misses him too much, David."

"I went down there to the beach, but he wouldn't say a word about Charlie. He tried to introduce me to his imaginary friends instead."

The father giant leaned forward in his chair and held the mother giant's hand in his own. "He used to be an ordinary kid playing catch on the beach with his best friend, and now he's out there talking to crickets and fireflies."

"Everyone needs friends, David."

"Real friends, Beth. Actual friends. Human friends. Not crickets and fireflies."

Cricket and Firefly waited for the mother and father giant to say something else, but neither of them did. After a while the father giant got up and cleared the table and began to wash the dishes. The mother giant dried them and put them away.

Firefly pushed off into the dark air, down the shore to the boat hidden behind the tiger lilies. Cricket leaped along beneath her.

Deep in the woods, the clearing was already bright with fireflies, and cricket music rose around them. Just then Firefly missed her nation. She missed swooping out of the knothole and gathering in the clearing with her friends. She missed daring them to go higher than the first branch. She missed trying to shock them into forgetting how to fly, and then hearing the *thud, thud, thud* all around her.

More than anything, she missed Elder. She looked up at the sky, glittering with stars. Which one was he? Was there any way to know?

When I fly up there, maybe I can find him, she thought.

But how would she know which star was Elder?

Below her, Cricket hopped along in time to the music. For a minute he wished he was singing too. His life would be simpler if he was still in school. If he could have just made himself sit dutifully through Telling Temperature and High Jumping and Fear of Giants class, if he hadn't stormed out that day, Cricket could be out there with the other crickets now, making music in the night. He even sort of missed Teacher.

But not as much as he missed Gloria.

He pictured her, her blue-green eyes, her desk and chair in the far corner, the way she had told him to go, told him to be free, told him to escape for the both of them. It was because of Gloria that he had come so far, he told himself—further than any other cricket had ever come—with his catching. He reminded himself of that. But still. It wasn't easy.

Just then, above him in the sky, he could have sworn that Firefly sighed.

They came to the fork in the path. If Firefly flew straight and Cricket turned left, they would end up not at Vole's boat but at their separate nations. Firefly slowed and Cricket paused. From the woods and marsh rose the song of the crickets, and the glow of the fireflies lit the deep woods.

After a moment, they looked at each other.

Then Firefly gave a single mighty pump of her wings.

Cricket crouched, all six legs tensed, and then sprang into the air.

"We're back!" called Firefly, swooping through the open galley window.

Cricket leaped nimbly—one, two, three—from the shore to the top of the tallest tiger lily to the deck, and then into the living room, where Vole, twig broom in paw, was sweeping the floor. A leaf full of minced tubers and fried fish waited for Cricket and Firefly on the wooden table, next to the old paper boat.

CHAPTER TWENTY-THREE

THE NEW GIANTS

The getaway raft was ready for final inspection. Cricket leaped its length and width several times, counting to make sure that each side of the raft was composed of an equal number of leaps.

"One, two, three," he murmured under his breath. "Four, five, six."

Peter sat back and watched nervously as Cricket circumnavigated the raft. After the third time around,

Cricket stopped. Out of breath, he nodded to Peter. The raft had been measured by Cricket, and no creatures were better at measuring than crickets.

Then it was Firefly's turn. Peter held tight to the mooring rope and let the raft drift into the current while Firefly flew back and forth above it from a height three times as tall as Peter. Her job was to note any places where the bound driftwood rode too low in the water. This was where Firefly's keen vision proved invaluable.

"There," she called, pointing with one wing, "and there, and there."

Once Peter hauled the raft back to shore and rein-forced its weak places with additional driftwood, the raft was finished. Enormous though it might be, it was beau-tiful. Its twine knots were tight and secure. The red bal-loon atop the fishing-pole mast bobbed in the morning breeze. And the blue stars blanket flag, and the yellow rubber ducky made it cozy and inviting.

"Now for the final touch!" said Peter, and he unloaded

the brown paper grocery bag he had lugged down to the shore.

A bag of oyster crackers.

A bottle of chocolate milk.

Three carrots.

An apple.

"That should do it," he said, and he stood back to admire the raft. "We're ready."

"What are we ready for, exactly?" said Cricket.

"To make our getaway," said Peter.

Just then there was a sound, a grinding noise, from the far bend of the road. All three of them turned to look.

The strange noise grew louder and louder and louder until a huge truck, enormous even by giant standards, hove into view. It trundled past Peter's driveway, and came to a shuddering halt by the empty giants' house down the road from the boy's house.

This was something entirely new.

Then came the sound of thunder. Cricket glanced up

at the sky, but it was cloudless, the dark blue of late summer. He looked back down the road, toward the empty giants' house. Ah. The back of the enormous truck was rolling up into the roof. The truck was full of giant furniture and boxes. Boxes and boxes and boxes.

Three unfamiliar giants jumped down from the high cab and tromped around to the yawning-open back of the truck. They shouted to one another in voices so deep and loud—

OUCH—

—that Cricket and Firefly both clapped wings over ears. Giants! So loud!

Peter didn't move at all. He stood absolutely still, watching.

Another sound of thunder, but this time it was a ramp that one of the new giants pulled down from the back of the truck. One giant thudded up the ramp into the shadowy interior, the second stood at the bottom of the ramp, and the third halfway to the house. The first one began hauling boxes out two at a time. He thunked down the ramp and handed them to the second giant, who turned and tromped them over to the third giant. The third giant propped open the door to the empty house with the first two boxes.

The assembly line picked up speed. These giants were fast despite their massive size. Boxes and boxes, two at a time, disappeared into the interior of the empty giants' house. Cricket and Firefly watched, wings still protecting their ears, until all the boxes had disappeared from the truck and were in the house.

Then the giants began unloading the furniture.

Despite her best efforts, Firefly trembled.

Cricket knew how she felt. All six of his legs were tensed.

After many weeks of spying on the giants, Firefly and Cricket were almost used to the hugeness of their kitchen table and their four-legged chairs and their hearth with its dark, enormous pit.

But to see the size of giant furniture now, in the stark light of day, was shocking. The three new giants abandoned their assembly line and moved each piece of furniture together, their muscles straining. Grunts and groans rose from their bent bodies as they struggled inside the house and then out again, straightening their backs, rolling their necks, shaking out their arms.

"You know what this means?" said Cricket suddenly.

"Of course I do," said Firefly, who didn't.

"It means that a new giant family is moving in," said Cricket. "Just like the mother and father giant said."

Peter said nothing. He didn't correct them the way he usually did—*they're not giants; they're my parents*—because he was still staring in the direction of the truck.

Just then an unfamiliar car came humming around the bend. As it approached the road where they stood watching, a blinking light appeared. Firefly scowled. She despised giant-made sources of light. So bright, so unvarying. So monotonous. So unlike the dancing, moving light of a firefly.

Peter still said nothing.

The car turned onto their road and slowed. Gravel spurted from under its wheels. It was a brown car, dusty-sided.

Whoosh!

As it passed, Cricket and Firefly huddled into themselves and covered their heads with their wings. No matter how good Cricket had gotten at catching, he was no match for a single piece of gravel flung from the wheel of a moving car.

The car slowed and slowed and slowed, and then it stopped. Cricket and Firefly held their breath as the two front doors of the dusty-sided brown car opened simultaneously.

"Giants," whispered Firefly. "*More* giants."

I told you so, thought Cricket, but he said nothing. Firefly squinted. A tall male giant. A slightly less tall female giant of the same age.

"A father giant," said Firefly.

"And a mother giant," said Cricket.

More giants, right here, right in Firefly Hollow. Then one of the back doors of the dusty-sided car opened, and they watched in silence as yet another giant emerged. Except this one wasn't a giant.

This one was a boy.

CHAPTER TWENTY-FOUR

WHAT DO THEY DO IN GIANT SCHOOL?

C*link. Clink.*

    Gulp. Gulp.

    Clink. Scrape. Gulp.

"So the new family is here?" said the father giant.

"They're here," said the mother giant.

"Did you meet them yet?"

"Not yet. They just moved in this morning. I thought I'd make them a cake tomorrow, as a welcome-to-the-neighborhood gift."

The father giant cleared his throat. The sound was so loud and gruesome, even through the window, that Firefly and Cricket cowered on their spy perch.

"And did I hear right, son?" he said. "Do they really have a boy your age?"

"Yeah."

"Maybe you two can be friends."

"No thanks."

The father giant sighed. The mother giant turned to the boy.

"Maybe you can be friends with Cricket and Firefly *and* the new boy."

Clink. Scrape. Gulp.

"Nope," said the boy. "Two friends are enough for me."

The father giant cleared his throat again. The awful sound was nearly enough to tumble Cricket right off the window ledge.

"Look, Peter," the father giant said. "School starts next week."

"Not for me it doesn't."

"Peter."

"David," said the mother giant. "Shh."

"Yeah," whispered Firefly to Cricket. "Shhh."

She fluttered up and down to keep warm. The chill in the air was unmistakable. Soon the leaves would turn red and gold and brown. The first frost would come, and then the first snow. The cricket and firefly nations would settle in for their long sleeps.

Not me, she thought. *Not Peter and Cricket and me, the nation of three.*

Cricket hopped back and forth on the window frame to keep warm. For a minute he thought of the School for Young Crickets. It was always warm in school. Then he pushed the image out of his mind. *Be tough, Cricket.*

Peter pushed back his chair: *SCRAPE.* Both Firefly and Cricket winced.

"So loud," Firefly said.

"Yeah," said Cricket. "It's as if he got bigger and louder overnight."

Cricket sounded like an elder, thought Firefly, always warning them about how giants got bigger before your very eyes. The front door opened, and there was Peter.

"He *looks* the same," said Firefly, and Cricket agreed.

Then, down the road, the door to the other giants' house opened, and the new miniature giant came outside. This one didn't leap out the door the way Peter did. His head was down and he moved slowly.

"Look how the new boy walks," said Firefly.

"He's a trudger," said Cricket.

"He'll be going to school."

"Yup. He's definitely the school type."

Just then the trudger lifted his head and looked at Peter.

"Hi," he said.

Cricket froze and Firefly stilled herself, moving her wings just enough to stay aloft. Peter said nothing.

"What's your name?" said the trudger, and he shuffled his feet forward until he stood only a few yards away from them.

This new boy's voice was higher and lighter than Peter's. He didn't look too dangerous, but Cricket didn't want to take any chances. He backed up slowly, very slowly, away from the new boy. He backed up and up until he backed straight into a thistle bush. *Ouch.* He rubbed his backside with one wing.

"I'm Jack," the new boy said when Peter didn't answer. "We just moved in."

He turned and pointed at the house where all the commotion had been, then turned back again. But in the second it took to turn and turn back, Peter ran away from the new boy, down the sand to the ancient white birch where Vole's boat was moored. Firefly and Cricket followed him. The new boy took a step after them, then hesitated. He turned away and walked back to his house.

Peter picked up a stone and tossed it into the river: *plop*. He tossed another, and another. Cricket watched the stones fly up into the air and fall into the water and disappear. If he were bigger, he could catch those stones.

Peter picked up another stone: *plop*. Then he crouched down in front of the clump of tiger lilies. He picked up a stick and scratched some giant letters into the sand:

Charlie

"What does that spell?" said Cricket.

But Peter didn't answer.

That night Vole lit his lantern and hung it from the mast. Then he went back into his living room, where the fire flickered in the hearth and the air was warm and smelled of smoke and fish and other good things, and while he waited for the little creatures to return from the shore, he practiced. He had made it all the way through the chart to the rolling hitch, a hitch that could be used to adjust and tighten a rope under tension. The rolling hitch was the kind of knot that would be especially useful in strong currents, thought Vole.

But how could he know for sure?

You can't, he told himself. *You just have to do the best you can.*

The day was finally coming when Vole would untie the rope that moored his boat to the big white birch. When he would finally know the motion of the boat on the open water. When the current would bear him south, down the long winding river, to where the river met the sea.

He wasn't ready, not yet. That much he knew. But he was getting close. All these long years, teaching himself how to sail from the diagrams and charts and knotted lengths of rope that his grandfather had left behind, were soon to be put to use. He would put himself to the test.

Would he, Vole, prove himself worthy of the river vole nation? He didn't want to fail his ancestors.

Vole's paws moved swiftly in his lap. After the rolling hitch, he had only the figure eight left to learn. The figure eight was a stopper knot used at the end of a line to keep it from sneaking away. Vole didn't know when, exactly, a stopper knot would be useful, but surely it would. His grandfather's voice, as it often did, came back to him.

You'll know, Vole. When the time is right, you'll know.

Then Cricket leaped onto the deck and bounded into the living room. Firefly whizzed through the open galley window and darted back and forth above the wooden table.

"The new boy's a trudger," Cricket told Vole.

Firefly zoomed up to the living room ceiling and then down again, narrowly missing the bow of the old paper boat.

"He'll be going to school for sure," said Firefly. "Peter says so too."

She zoomed up to the ceiling again and did a little twirl

by the mantelpiece. Cricket reared back on his hind legs and raised both wings, as if he were about to make an extraordinary catch.

"What do they *do* in giant school, anyway?" said Firefly.

"Well, they're not crickets," said Cricket, "so they can't have High Jumping class. And they're already giants, so they can't have Fear of Giants class."

"Forget about aerial maneuvers and endurance flying," added Firefly.

"They learn about giant things," said Vole. "They learn how to do numbers."

"I know how to do numbers," said Cricket. "I know how to tell the temperature."

"And they learn how to read," said Vole. "They learn how to write."

Firefly hovered above the paper boat, looking down at Cricket, whose wings were still raised, waiting for an imaginary catch.

"Who needs to know how to read and write?" she said.

"Yeah," said Cricket. "Who needs that kind of thing?"

"If we knew how to read," said Vole, pointing to the paper boat, "we'd know what those letters said."

Cricket lowered himself onto all six legs and peered up at the paper boat. He thought of the letters that Peter had scratched into the sand with a stick. Firefly floated alongside him, brushing the old boat with her wing. What *did* those letters say? The words of the elders echoed in her mind: *Miniature giants are nothing but future giants.*

"Vole?" said Firefly. "Was your boy like Peter?"

"In some ways."

"Did he like to play catch?" said Cricket.

"He did."

"Did you play catch with him?"

Vole shook his head. He spread his paws out in front of him. They were so big, thought Cricket, but they were still much smaller than a giant's hands. Vole probably couldn't catch anything bigger than an oak seed either. Maybe an acorn, but that would be pushing it.

"Did you love him the way we love Peter?" said Firefly.

Vole nodded. Firefly sighed. Cricket sighed. Theirs were tiny sighs, because they were so small. Still, though, the flames in the fireplace shivered a little.

CHAPTER TWENTY-FIVE

SCHOOL, SCHOOL, SCHOOL

L ike it or not, Peter, September is just around the corner," said the father giant. "And that means school."

Outside, on the window ledge, Cricket and Firefly rolled their eyes at each other. Did these giants never tire of talking about school, school, school?

"I'm not going," said Peter.

Clunk. The father giant set his fork down hard on the wooden table.

"You can't just spend your days on the river building rafts and playing catch with imaginary creatures."

"David," said the mother giant. "Let it alone."

Peter pushed back his chair. *Scrape. Tromp. Splash.* And he was gone, running down the hall to his room. The window frame trembled from the force of his footfalls.

"David, don't you remember being his age?" said the mother giant. "Don't you remember wanting a best friend? A kindred spirit?"

"Yes," said the father giant. "Of course. But this imaginary friend thing has gone on far too long."

"But you had one too. For quite a while, your mother said. And yet you eventually left him behind."

The father giant pushed back from the table—*scrape, tromp*—and then water began splashing in the sink.

"The time has to be right," said the mother giant. "Peter will know when it's time."

The father giant said nothing.

What's a kindred spirit? thought Firefly. She looked down at Cricket.

"Cricket, do you think that Peter will leave us behind?" she said. "Do you think it could be true?"

"No," said Cricket.

But the window frame felt cold under his legs, and he shivered. Together they made their way back down the shore to the boat, moored to the white pine. The night air was chilly, and Firefly tried to curl her legs up around herself for warmth, but that was hard to do in midair. Then she tried to wrap her wings around herself. That was a big mistake.

"What are you doing?" said Cricket, staring up at her in alarm. "Forgetting how to fly?"

"No. Just trying to stay warm."

"Well, stop it. I don't want you falling on top of me."

Firefly straightened out her legs and wings and rolled over onto her back. The sun had just set, and there was no moon yet. When would it come out? Where did the moon go during the day? Was it cold up there?

She rolled back over on her stomach and hung in the air, looking down at Cricket.

"Cricket?"

"What?"

"Do you ever miss the cricket nation?"

He took a big leap forward. "Nope."

"Never?"

"Nope."

But he was lying.

"Cricket?"

"Now what?"

"I don't miss the firefly nation either."

But she was lying too. She did miss the firefly nation, and she missed Elder more.

"Cricket?"

"WHAT?"

"I'm going to go practice my upward zooms."

"Now? In the dark?"

"Yeah. The dark didn't stop the giants, did it?"

No, thought Cricket. But Firefly wasn't a giant, and she didn't have a silver spaceship. Still, he said, "Well, okay. If you have to. I'll see you back at the boat."

"Okay," said Firefly, and she flew off into the night to practice her upward zooms.

But she didn't.

What she did was wait until Cricket had hopped out of sight. Then she aimed herself toward the clearing, where the firefly nation was gathering, and she took off, flying fast, before she lost her courage, zooming toward the tree where she had been born and where Elder had saved her life and taught her to fly in the first place. The young fireflies were swooping out of the knothole: one, two, three, and then too many to count. Firefly slowed as she got closer, and then she hid herself behind a big pinecone on a thick limb, so that none of them would see her.

Wow. Look at them go!

Firefly stared as the fireflies she remembered as being

timid and fearful twirled and darted about the clearing. She drifted to a closer pinecone and peeked around it.

"You're getting so much better at swoops," said one.

No kidding, thought Firefly. It amazed her how much better they all flew now, compared to the beginning of the summer.

"Do you really think so? I still wish my flip-arounds were faster."

"Practice makes perfect," said another. "Remember Firefly's swoops?"

"Hers were the best."

"Do you think she ever misses us?"

"No."

"She's probably forgotten all about us," said another.

"Where do you think she is now?"

"Gone."

"Gone where, though?"

"Up to the moon," said another, and laughed. "Maybe she got a ride with a giant."

Some of the others began to laugh too.

"In a silver spaceship."

Firefly trembled with anger. She had to stop herself from darting out from behind the pinecone and dive-bombing them. More fireflies joined in the laughter. But not all of them.

"Don't you miss her, though?" said one. "Even a little?"

The laughter died down. Young fireflies floated in the air of the clearing.

"No," said one.

"Not really," said another.

They didn't miss her? At all? Firefly's gut hurt as if she had been punched. Now she couldn't hold herself back.

"You don't miss me?" she yelled from behind the pinecone. "Well, guess what? I don't miss you, either!"

And she darted out into their midst.

Thud. Thud. Thud.

Three of them folded their wings up in shock and

plopped straight to the ground. Firefly was still so angry she could barely see straight.

"Good-bye," she said. "I don't care if I never get back."

She arrowed herself toward the river and took off.

CHAPTER TWENTY-SIX

A LONELY FEELING

C ricket crouched alone on the riverbank. The clearing was brighter than usual. He looked in the other direction, toward the open field and the road that the father giant roared down every morning. Firefly was out there somewhere, practicing her upward zooms.

The music of the cricket nation rose from the marsh and the fields and the woods. *Chirrup, chirrup, chirrup,* to a steady beat. Cricket hopped slowly down the sand to the big rock.

Sproing!

He stood there, the breeze off the river blowing his antennae back. He raised his wings and rubbed them together.

> *"Take me out to the ball game*
> *Take me out with the crowd.*
> *Buy me some peanuts and Cracker Jack*
> *I don't care if I never get back."*

But was that really true?

Cricket imagined leaving Firefly Hollow for parts unknown. He imagined sailing away on the getaway raft, for example, down around the bend of the river and beyond. He imagined never seeing the fireflies again, glowing deep in the woods in the clearing by the hollow tree. Never leaping to the window frame of the giants' kitchen to spy on them. Never sneaking into the Museum of Giant Artifacts again, the better to stare at the photo of Yogi Berra, world's greatest catcher.

It was a lonely feeling.

Was this how Peter felt at the thought of never seeing Charlie again?

Was this how Firefly felt at the thought of never seeing Elder again?

Cricket hunched up low to the ground. He tried singing the last line of the song once more, very softly, to see how it felt.

"I don't care if I never get back."

Again he shivered. Enough of this. He leaped off the rock and straight down the shore to the clump of tiger lilies, and from there he jumped to the deck of the boat, where Vole was standing by the rudder, turning it back and forth.

"What are you doing?" said Cricket.

Vole looked up, startled, and dropped his paws from the rudder. "Nothing," he said.

"Vole? Are you going to sail away soon?"

Vole put his paws back on the rudder and began turning it again. "Maybe," he said. "When the time is right."

Oh no. First Charlie, and then Elder, and now Vole. Couldn't anything stay the same? Cricket sighed and closed his eyes. He leaned back on his four hind legs and raised his wings in the air. *Just one great catch,* he thought. *If only I could make just one great, non-dandelion-fluff catch.* He imagined a glowing white baseball, just like the one in the Museum of Giant Artifacts, coming at him out of a clear blue sky. Wait for it, wait for it, wait for it, tear off the catcher's mask and hold up the glove, and then—

Yes! Cricket has done it again! Have you ever seen a cricket catcher catch like that Cricket can catch? And the crowd goes wild!

Chirrup! Chirrup! Chirrup!

That was the sound of the crowd, exploding in applause for Cricket, Catcher Extraordinaire.

Cricket sank back down on his haunches and peered

around the deck. It was quiet. No one was cheering for him. There was only Vole, across the deck at the rudder, practicing how to sail. He glanced back at the path behind the boat. Not far away was the School for Young Crickets, empty at this time of night when all the crickets spread out in the fields and marsh and woods to chirrup their music to the night. Was Teacher out there? Was Gloria crouched before the window, listening to the others sing?

Cricket reared up on his hind legs again and turned his face to the moon. The moon looked a little like a baseball, didn't it? An outer space baseball. *Let it come to you,* he thought, and he held up his wings to the moon.

Oh, what was the use? Who was he trying to kid? All his baseballs were imaginary, because a real one would kill him.

"It's not fair," he said.

"What's not fair?" said Vole.

"That I can't catch like the giants can."

He dropped his head into his wings. He pictured the

Yogi Berra baseball card in the Museum of Giant Artifacts, and how it had entranced him the very first time he saw it. He thought of all the times he had crept down to the shore of the river and watched Peter and Charlie playing catch. He wanted that for himself.

But Cricket had wings, not arms.

He had six legs and a carapace instead of two legs and a bendable spine.

He had no hands at all, let alone opposable thumbs.

A summer of effort and all he had to show for it was dandelion fluff, caught and clasped between his wings. That, and a single maple leaf that had almost crushed him.

"It's not fair," he said again. "Why should giants be the only ones? If I could only make just one catch. Just one real, actual catch."

The giants' house was nearly invisible in the darkness. Firefly's question hung in his mind.

"Tell me something, Vole," he said. "Do boys really

grow into giants? Is Peter going to leave us behind?"

"Come into the living room with me, Cricket."

The ancient paper boat was in its place on top of the wooden table. Cricket had never seen Vole move it. There he stood, in the moonlight, his paw trailing along the side of the boat as if it were something precious. The black letters on the side stood out clearly—the moon was very bright tonight—and Cricket wished again that he knew how to read giant letters.

"You told us that your miniature giant made this boat for you," said Cricket. "But where is he now? Where did your miniature giant go?"

Somewhere off to the left an owl hooted, and a whip-poor-will called from its hiding place in the grasses by the river. Would another one answer?

Poor Will.

Yes.

Poor Will. Poor Will.

Back and forth went the whip-poor-wills in the

dark night, one in the grass by the river, the other off in the woods. Vole opened his mouth, as if he were about to answer the question, but then an unfamiliar sound—a vibration, or a buzz—came from deep within the woods, and both Cricket and Vole raced up to the deck.

The crickets were coming.

CHAPTER TWENTY-SEVEN

WE HAVE COME IN
SEARCH OF CRICKET

The hum of their voices, faint at first, grew ever louder. From the roots of trees, from under the overhanging rocks, from the tall grass and the edge of the marsh, the crickets were coming. One clear voice rang out above the others, counting out a marching beat.

"One and two and three and leap!
One and two and three and leap!"

"That's her," said Cricket to Vole. "That's Teacher, the one who wants to put me in detention for the rest of my life."

Teacher, whose stern and forbidding eyes had followed him every day of his young life at the School for Young Crickets. Her voice was the voice that led the crickets on. The ground trembled slightly under the weight of hundreds of crickets leaping in unison. On they came, and then they were there, at the bottom of the rope ladder that led up to the deck of the boat.

Vole leaned against the railing, his eyes fixed on the tall figure of Teacher. Cricket ducked down below the railing so that she wouldn't see him, then lifted his head ever so slightly and peeked out over the edge.

Teacher made a mighty leap onto the tallest tiger lily and reared back on her hind legs, keeping perfect balance. She met Vole's gaze head-on. A cricket clung to her back, and Cricket saw that it was Gloria.

Gloria!

Gloria, with her unearthly blue-green eyes. The other young crickets massed around them, silent.

"Mr. Vole," said Teacher.

"Ms. Teacher," said Vole.

"My students and I have come in search of Cricket."

"Why?"

Teacher balanced perfectly on her two hind legs, her wings half-raised in the air. Even though Vole towered above her, furry and enormous, her dark eyes were steady. She said nothing.

"Why?" repeated Vole.

Gloria clung to Teacher's back and stared at Vole. Her eyes glowed. Teacher didn't answer. *Be fearless,* thought Cricket, and he leaped out in front of tall Vole.

"Yeah, tell us why," he said. "So that you can put me in detention for the rest of my life? So that you can laugh at me some more?"

Teacher's eyes narrowed.

"I was trying to keep you safe," she said. "This fascination with giants and their giant ways can lead to no good."

Vole cleared his throat.

"You haven't answered my question, Ms. Teacher," said Vole. "Why do you want to find him?"

"Because," said one of the bolder of the young crickets.

"Yeah!" said the others. "Because!"

"Because why?"

Gloria, clinging precariously to Teacher's carapace, raised her good wing for attention.

"Because they miss him," she said. "That's why."

Chirrup! Chirrup! Chirrup!

Cricket stared down at the massed crickets.

"Yeah!"

"That's right!"

"We miss him!"

One started to chirp Cricket's baseball song. Then they all began to chirp and hop at once. The sand around the clump of tiger lilies vibrated beneath them. Teacher shook her head and sighed, as if she was giving up. She raised and lowered her wings.

"He's weird," said a cricket, "and he's a pain, but we miss him anyway."

"He keeps things interesting," said another.

Gloria's blue-green eyes shone up at Cricket's, and she smiled.

The light from the moon high above was steady, and the river water below twinkled in its path. Down on the sand the young crickets leaped and chirped. Suddenly Teacher raised a wing and turned her head in the direction of the forest. The young crickets turned too, and then they hushed.

From the woods came a faint glow. The forest was filling with light. Cricket poked Vole's furry leg with his wing.

"Fireflies," he whispered. "The fireflies are coming too."

They had left the safety of the clearing and were floating their way out of the forest to the banks of the river. They advanced through the dark air, a faint buzz surrounding them. Teacher and the rest of the crickets turned their heads in the direction of the light.

"What's going on?" Cricket said to Vole, but Vole shook his head.

"I don't know."

"Have you ever seen the fireflies leave the clearing before?"

"Never."

They stood still and watched. The sound now divided itself into distinct voices. Hundreds of fireflies called from the forest, hundreds of fireflies lit the night, and all were coming this way. Vole and Cricket stood on the deck of the boat, mesmerized by the growing light.

Cricket, with his sharp ears, was able to make out what they were saying first.

"No, Firefly!"

"Don't do it, Firefly!"

"Come back, Firefly!"

Cricket turned to Vole.

"It's Firefly," he said. "Something's wrong."

Vole gripped the railing with both paws. He tilted his furry head, the better to hear. Now the voices of the fireflies were clear and urgent.

"You'll fall!"

"You'll drop straight into the river!"

"You'll drown!"

The young crickets down on the sand leaped and buzzed anew, craning their heads at a strange, small light sparkling high in the inky sky.

"Look!"

"What *is* that?"

Cricket leaned back, the better to see it, and so did the others.

"It's Cricket's friend!" said a young cricket. "The crazy firefly!"

CHAPTER TWENTY-EIGHT

ONWARD

The cricket and firefly nations turned their heads to the sky in unison. There was Firefly, so high up that they could barely see her. They all fell silent, watching. Cricket crossed his wings for luck.

Far above, Firefly took a deep breath, spread her wings, and pushed them down in another mighty stroke. Up she zoomed, the cool night air rushing past her.

If the giants can do it, so can you, she told herself.

She leaned her head back and looked up at the moon. It was round as an owl's face, and the stars sparkled high above.

Elder's up there, she told herself. *All you have to do is keep going. One wing stroke at a time.*

That was how the giants did it. Well, maybe not exactly like that—they had their silver spaceships—but close.

Onward and upward she flew.

Perseverance, she told herself. *Determination.*

Zoom!

A faint sound reached her ears, and she glanced down. Spread out along the shoreline of the river, the light of what could only be fireflies shimmered and glowed. Had the fireflies come to watch her fly?

No. That couldn't be. They hadn't even missed her.

But what else could that light be? She stared down in surprise, for a moment almost forgetting to keep her wings moving. It *was* the fireflies. They had ventured out of the clearing, and they were watching her fly! This gave her extra strength. She forced her wings down with renewed determination.

Zoom!

Now she was higher than she'd ever been before. All that practice this summer had paid off.

But the higher she flew, the thinner the air. The thinner the air, the colder she felt. She wasn't used to feeling so cold, but she didn't turn back.

She decided to distract herself with star formations.

That one over there in the western sky looked like a fish, didn't it? She wondered what being a fish would be like.

It would mean being stuck underwater her whole life, for one thing. No thanks. Besides, fish couldn't fly.

That cluster of stars to the east looked like a bear. She and Cricket had glimpsed a bear once, a black bear eating blueberries by the edge of the woods. They had huddled together next to the raft underneath the big rock and watched the bear lumber from bush to bush, raking through the leaves and branches with his big paws, shoving them into his mouth. The bear stank of coarse fur and dirt and massive strength. He paid no attention to his surroundings, other than to shovel the blueberries into his mouth.

Would Firefly ever want to be a bear?

No. Too heavy and stinky.

And bears couldn't fly either.

She spread her wings wide and pushed down. Up she zoomed. Except that at this point it wasn't so much of a zoom as a float. The air up here was so thin, and she was tired. *Distract yourself,* she thought. *Keep on going.*

In the southern sky was a grouping of stars that looked a little like Vole.

She tried to imagine life as a river vole. She would live on Vole's boat and catch fish for her dinner. She would sit on his deck and watch the moonlight shimmering on the water.

That didn't seem so bad, did it?

But river voles couldn't fly either.

No thanks to being a river vole. She took a tiny break and lay on her back, staring up. Now, what was that, right above her to the left of the moon? That little group of stars looked just like Cricket when he was crouching, preparing to catch another dandelion fluff. *Wings up, Cricket,* she thought. *Let it come to you!*

She gathered her strength for another push upward when an entirely new thought came to her.

What if she could be a *giant?*

Imagine being a giant. Imagine having that enormous body, those enormous arms and legs and hands and feet. Those enormous eyes. That enormous house. Think how powerful she would be, if she were a giant. The earth would tremble from her footfalls. All creatures would quake before her.

It was an entrancing thought.

But if she were a giant, she would have to live in a house. She would have to go to school. She would have to eat that awful giant food. She would be a wingless creature, dependent on a silver spaceship to fly up to the moon. And while the giants had landed on the moon, and even walked around on it, they hadn't stayed there, had they?

She flipped over, spread her wings, and pushed downward. But the air was awfully thin up here, and she gained only a few inches of altitude. She tipped her head back and stared at the fat yellow moon. It didn't look any closer at all. How had the giants done it?

Firefly was so tired. Maybe she could rest again for a minute. Even a few seconds would help.

She turned on her back once more and sought out the group of stars that reminded her of Cricket. *Cricket, Catcher Extraordinaire,* she thought, and suddenly her heart hurt.

I miss you, Cricket, she thought. And then, *I miss you, Vole. I miss you, Peter.*

Firefly flipped onto her stomach, fluttering her wings just enough to stay aloft. Far, far below shone the blue-

green earth. Look at it. There was the green land, and the blue oceans. If she looked hard enough, could she see the river? Could she see Firefly Hollow? She marshaled all her powers of concentration.

Oh, there it was. There was the woods, and the river sparkling beside it, and the dark hulk of Peter's house.

Onward, she thought. *Onward and upward.*

She forced her wings open and then down. It was strange to be flying alone like this, instead of hovering low to the earth, just above Cricket. She gave herself an extra push, so that she would zoom up again.

But there was no zoom. The air was so very thin. She'd had no idea that the air itself changed when you got so high. She was probably the only living firefly who knew this. All the others were too afraid to fly this high.

She could see why, too. It was hard to breathe, way up here.

She felt dizzy.

And faint.

Firefly took a huge breath, trying to fill her lungs, but she couldn't. She spread her wings and gathered her strength, trying for another mighty stroke, but she couldn't. The stars didn't seem as bright as they had when she began flying to the top of the sky, and the moon wobbled when she looked up at it to get her bearings.

For a minute she thought of Vole's cozy fireplace. She thought of the hollow tree in which she had been born and learned to fly. She thought of Elder, who understood her.

Oh, how cold it was up here.

She couldn't breathe.

"Elder, help me," she whispered into the thin air.

I'll be watching over you, came his voice in her ears.

In the faint hope that he might answer, she mustered the last of her energy and blinked out their secret code—*fast fast fast, looooong loooooong*—but there was no corresponding blink from the stars above. Firefly looked down.

The cricket and firefly nations were amassed far, far below on the shore. Even from this distance the light from the fireflies was visible, and the dark eyes of the crickets glowed up at her. She could even see the dim light of Vole's fireplace, glowing behind the tiger lilies.

It was a bewitching sight. She had never realized just how beautiful it was down there. She hung motionless in space for a while, looking down. But she couldn't breathe, and stars swam in her head now. She couldn't move her wings anymore.

The time isn't right, she thought. *I want to go home.*

Her last act before darkness overcame her was to let her wings float up above her head in parachute formation. Then she began to fall—

—down

    and down

        and dooooooooooooooown.

CHAPTER TWENTY-NINE

DISTANT VOICES WERE CALLING

In the giants' house, Peter sat on the floor of his bedroom in his starship pajamas, the stack of fresh school paper before him and a new, sharpened pencil in his hand. Page after page filled with the same letters:

I miss Charlie.
I miss Charlie.
I miss Charlie.

Over and over and over he wrote. After a while his hand moved automatically, and the words became easier and easier to write. He was so absorbed in his task that for a long time he didn't notice what was happening outside, down on the shore. Only when the moonlight outside grew so bright that his window filled with light did he hear the commotion and look up. He got up and went to his window and pressed his nose against the screen. Small, distant voices were calling.

"No, Firefly!"

"Don't do it!"

"You'll drown!"

The light of a thousand fireflies glowed on the shore, and the very air vibrated and buzzed from a swarm of crickets, leaping and chirruping on the sand.

Peter raced to the closed door of his bedroom, yanked it open, and pounded down the hall. Through the kitchen and past the surprised faces of his parents, who stood at the sink doing dishes.

"It's Firefly," he yelled in answer to their *Wait, where are you going?* questions. "She's in trouble!"

And out the door he ran.

The creatures down below watched in horror as Firefly began to fall. Those who had cheered her ascent now watched in silence as she pinwheeled through space like a tiny falling star. The amassed crickets held their collective breath and turned their heads to the heavens, and the firefly nation barely stayed aloft in the air.

They were all frozen in place, intent on Firefly's descent.

Then Peter, his parents far behind him, came pounding down the shore.

"Cricket!" he shouted. "Where are you?"

Cricket was still crouched on the deck of the boat, unable to tear his eyes away from the sight of Firefly falling from the sky. The sound of Peter's voice jolted him from his trance.

"Peter!" he yelled back, his heart pounding.
"It's Firefly! She's falling!"

"I know! We have to rescue her!"

Peter raced to the raft and heaved it from its
storage place by the big rock and began hauling
it down to the water.

"Hurry, Cricket!"

Cricket came alive.

Sproing!

With one giant leap he sprang off the boat
and halfway to the raft. Peter stood in the water,
his starship pajamas getting wet, one hand holding
the raft steady and the other hand on the red-balloon
mast.

"Get on!" he said. "We've got to catch her!"

Cricket leaped aboard and steadied himself on the
rubber duck's neck. He looked up. There she was, still
falling. Still pinwheeling through the dark sky, straight
toward the river. All the dire predictions of the cricket

and firefly nations jumbled together in his mind in a big heap of worry.

Water is to be feared.

You will drown.

No firefly has ever flown that high.

Certain failure.

Doomed.

"You ready?" said Peter.

No. Cricket wasn't ready. He would never be ready. This was craziness, he saw now, pure craziness. He didn't know how to swim. Teacher was right. If the raft tipped over, he would drown immediately.

"Cricket!" said Peter.

But what choice did Cricket have? Firefly was still falling. Her wings were held out to her sides, the wind rushing beneath them. She was headed directly toward the middle of the river, where the water was deep and swift. It was now or never.

"Ready," said Cricket.

And with that, Peter pushed off from the shore and leaped aboard. Cricket clung to the rubber duck's neck with all six legs and folded his wings tight to his body, the better to hold on.

"Peter!"

"Peter!"

Cricket peered back. Oh no. The mother and father giants were at the river's edge now, and the father giant had already stepped into the water.

"We have to save Firefly!" Peter shouted back to them, and he poled the raft farther out into the water.

Back onshore, the cricket and firefly nations buzzed and blinked. Crickets leaped about in a chaos of sound, and the fireflies rose higher into the air, flickering back and forth, a frantic mass.

"Peter!" shouted the giants.

"Firefly!" called the fireflies.

"Cricket!" yelled the crickets.

Cricket held on to the duck's neck for dear life and

kept his head craned back, eyes on Firefly. She fell through moonlight that shone down like a spotlight, illuminating her path. Then—

Crunch.

The raft jolted alarmingly, and one corner sank. The plastic milk jug came undone, its twine tie floating downstream before their eyes. The knots were coming undone. The edge of the raft was sinking. Now it was submerged. Now the raft itself was taking on water. Peter stopped poling and bent down. He cupped his enormous hands together and flung water back into the river. But it was no use. The raft was going under.

CHAPTER THIRTY

HANG ON!

I n desperation, Cricket turned back toward the shore.

"Vole!" he shouted. "Voooooooole!"

There was an enormous splashing. The father giant was in the river and upon them. He scooped Peter up and turned toward the shore, Peter struggling in his arms.

Vole heard Cricket's cries from the deck of the boat where he stood, also frozen. He had watched the entire scene with horror. Firefly was still falling, and there was no sign that she would regain consciousness in time to stop herself. The young fireflies below were crying now.

"No, Firefly, no," they moaned.

Vole shut his eyes for a moment, sickened as the memory of the flood came rushing back over him. He had lost everything that night: his grandfather, his friends, his entire way of life. Everything.

No, he thought then, *not everything.*

Vole opened his eyes and pushed himself away from the railing.

"I'm coming!" he heard himself shout. "Hang on!"

Vole had never moved so fast in his life. *Remember what you've learned,* he told himself, *remember.* Around the deck to the mooring rope he ran, and he knelt on his hind paws and tried desperately to undo the knot. But it was swollen by many years of water and disuse. Vole grabbed his filet knife and sawed through the dense twine. He used all his strength, and the twine broke free.

You'll know when the time is right, his grandfather had said.

Now was the time. The boat leaped away from the shore as if it had been waiting for this moment, its sail catching the breeze and puffing out white and full. Vole ran to the rudder and began tacking to the sinking raft, using the maneuvers he had taught himself from the *River Vole's Guide.*

Now he saw the outline of Cricket, clinging fast to the neck of the rubber duck.

"Hang on, Cricket!" he called, and he glanced up at the heavens.

Firefly was close now. So close. The fireflies and crickets began to chant in unison.

"Save her!"

"Save her!"

"Save her!"

On the shore, Peter's parents knelt with their backs to Cricket, their arms around their son, trying to soothe him. Peter shook with sobs, trying to break free.

"Don't let her die!" he screamed. "Don't let her die!"

Vole was only a foot away from Cricket now. He held on to the rudder with one paw and extended the other to Cricket, but the little cricket shook his head. He was paralyzed with fear, clinging to the duck's neck.

Vole took a deep breath, calmed his voice, and aimed it directly at Cricket.

"This is it, Cricket," he said. "You can do this. You can make the catch."

At that, Cricket stared at Vole, his dark eyes glowing. *You can do this. You can make the catch.* His legs loosened on the duck's neck.

"There's no time left," said Vole. "Don't think. Just do it."

Cricket jumped off the rubber duck's neck and landed lightly on the deck of the boat. He glanced up and crouched down. Above him glimmered a thousand stars, but he paid no attention to their twinkling. He kept his

eyes steady on the tiny firefly floating her way toward him out of the dark.

Let it come to you, he chanted silently. *Let it come to you.*

Keep your eye on the ball. Keep your eye on the ball.

The cricket and firefly nations watched from the shore. Peter stopped struggling against his parents' arms and held his breath. Firefly, unconscious, drifted down on the breeze. A little to the left—and Cricket leaped, and now a little to the right—and Cricket leaped, and now back again.

At the exact right moment, he extended his wings and adjusted his footing.

And Firefly fell straight into his wings.

CHAPTER THIRTY-ONE

IS SHE BREATHING?

The world around Cricket and Vole silenced itself, as if every living being in Firefly Hollow were holding its breath at the same time, waiting for Firefly to wake up.

Vole maneuvered the boat back to its hidden berth behind the clump of lilies and dropped anchor in the shallows. His heart pounded. *She needs air,* he told himself, *air and space.* He scooped up both Cricket and

Firefly in his shaking paws and carried them gently to a smooth patch of sand.

The fireflies amassed above them, a column of light that lit the sand.

"I missed her so much," one of them wept. "I never told her I missed her."

"Neither did I," said another one.

"Me either," said a third.

The crickets hopped and leaped their way down the shore and gathered beside them. Teacher stood on her hind legs, taller than all the others, Gloria still piggy-backed on her carapace.

Everyone waited.

Down the shore, Peter cried and cried.

"Don't be dead," he cried. "Please, Firefly, don't be dead."

He broke free of his parents and ran down the beach, the mother and father giant following. The three of them stopped on the shore, Peter pushing his way into the crowd next to Firefly, his parents looking in dismay at the raft.

"He's so upset—he spent weeks working on that raft," said the mother giant, "and now it's sinking."

"Should we try to save it?" said the father giant.

The mother giant nodded. "I'll go get the duck and the ball," she said, wading into the water, "and you go after the raft."

And off they went, never noticing the little creatures gathered on the sand, intent on Firefly.

"Is she dead?" said Peter.

"We don't know," said a cricket.

"We hope not," said a firefly.

There's a miniature giant right next to us, thought the fireflies and crickets then, *and he sees us and hears us.*

On an ordinary night, this would be astonishing. But this was not an ordinary night. No one said anything else. Everyone watched and waited as Cricket unclenched his wings. There, on their glimmering outstretched length, lay Firefly. She was a crumpled ball, her wings still folded tight to her body. Her eyes were closed.

Peter reached out his enormous pinkie finger and stroked Firefly's belly. Nothing. The cricket and firefly nations drew closer. Peter stroked her belly again: nothing.

Then he began to whisper the baseball song.

"Take me out to the ball game
Take me out with the crowd.
Buy me some peanuts and Cracker Jack
I don't care if I never get back."

Firefly's eyes opened. She stared up, first at Cricket, then around her. Then she tried to sit up and realized that Cricket was holding her in his wings.

"What are you all doing here?" she said.

At that, the firefly and cricket nations let out their collective breath. All around rose the sound of their voices: "She's alive. Firefly's alive."

It was at that moment that Cricket realized exactly what had happened. He'd caught her. He'd caught her! He, Cricket, had held out his wings to Firefly, falling from the sky, and just when it seemed that she would fall straight into the river and drown, he had caught her. This was the catch of his life.

I did it. I did it.

Was this what it felt like to be Yogi Berra?

No. This was better.

He felt a furry paw on his shoulder. Cricket looked up. Vole towered above the cricket nation. But even standing on his hind legs, he came only to Peter's ankle. Next to Peter, the boat, bobbing lightly on the water, looked like a little paper boat.

"You did it, Cricket," said Vole.

"You did it too, Vole," said Cricket.

"You did what?" said Firefly. "Vole did what?"

She struggled again to sit up, and this time she managed. Then she spread her wings, flexed them, and tried to hoist herself into the air. But she was exhausted beyond measure, and she slipped to the ground and rested on the sand instead.

"Cricket caught you," said Vole.

"Vole untied the boat," said Cricket.

"What are you *talking* about?" said Firefly. "Cricket can't catch anything but dandelion fluff. And Vole never unties the boat."

"He did tonight," said Vole and Cricket together, pointing to each other.

Firefly shook her head, trying to take it all in. She looked down the beach. Peter and the creatures followed her gaze to the mother and the father giants, who were wading back out of the river, empty-handed. All that remained of the raft was the red balloon, bobbing on the surface of the waves. Firefly's eyes widened. Everything seemed to come back to her at once, and she struggled up to her feet, her spindly legs wobbling beneath her.

"I was trying to fly up to the moon," she said. "But I failed, didn't I?"

One of the elders floated forward and cleared her throat.

"No, Firefly," she said. "You didn't fail. You flew. Farther than any of us thought possible."

With that, the smallest of the fireflies pushed forward through the crowd and hovered above Firefly.

"I missed you!" he said. "I was just about to say that when you took off."

"Me too," said another firefly. "It's boring without you around. I'm glad you're not dead."

And they all began to talk at once. Firefly looked at them in wonder. She remembered flying up and up and up. She remembered being cold. She remembered stars gathering inside her head. She remembered the sound of Elder's voice in her head: *I'll be watching over you.* She remembered, at the very end, spreading her wings out wide in parachute formation.

Peter rose to his feet and stepped back a few paces. He took in the whole scene. Fireflies buzzed and blinked as they darted back and forth. Crickets leaped and chirped on the sand, cheering in unison.

"Cri-cket!"

"Cri-cket!"

"Cri-cket!"

Then Peter watched as the red balloon broke free from the sunken raft and skimmed away, tugged this way and that on the air currents, until it passed around the bend and disappeared from sight.

The getaway raft was gone.

Charlie was gone.

But Firefly was alive.

Firefly flapped her wings experimentally and lifted herself into the air. She hovered in front of Peter's face.

"It's not true, you know," she said.

"What's not true?"

"The part in the song that says you don't care if you never get back."

She did a loop-de-loop around his head, and then she butted him gently on the nose. "I cared," she said, before she flew back to the fireflies and crickets.

Peter turned and ran to his parents, who were waiting on the sand and watching him anxiously.

"We couldn't save the raft, honey," said his mother.

"I'm sorry, buddy," said his father. "I tried to grab it, but it was too late."

"Charlie's gone forever," said Peter.

"Yes," said his father. "He is."

Peter nodded once, and then he took a deep breath.

"Okay," he said.

"Okay what?" said his father.

"Okay," said Peter. "I'll go back to school."

CHAPTER THIRTY-TWO

THE GRINDING SOUND OF THE SCHOOL BUS

The morning after Cricket's great catch, the chill in the air was unmistakable.

Soon would come the first hard frost, and then snow would not be far behind. There would be many months of no cricket song, no soft glow in the clearing. Stillness would settle over Firefly Hollow.

The getaway raft was gone.

Peter was going to school.

Firefly and Cricket, battered and bruised, huddled by the rock, listening to Peter's footsteps—*pound, pound, pound*—coming down the hall in the giants' house. They waited while he ate his cereal—*clink, clink, clink*—and then pushed back his chair—*scrape*—and put his bowl in the sink—*thunk*—and ran water into it—*sssssssss*.

Then he came out the front door. At the exact same time, the door to the other giants' house opened, and the new boy, Jack, came trudging out. Peter looked at Firefly and Cricket and gave them a tiny wave. Then he turned to Jack.

"Hi," he said. "I'm Peter."

The new boy's face lit up in a smile. He stubbed the toe of his sneaker in the dirt and then looked straight at Peter.

"Who were you waving at?" he said.

"My friends."

"Where?" said Jack. "I don't see anyone."

"They're right there."

"A cricket and a bug?" Jack said, pointing.

"Yeah. That's them."

The new boy tilted his head.

"I heard about your other friend," he said. "Charlie. Did you used to play together a lot?"

"Yeah."

"I could play with you," offered Jack. "If you want, I mean."

"Maybe," said Peter.

Down the sand, the boat moored once again to the white birch, Vole watched the scene unfold. He watched as the boys, their heads down, began to talk. He watched as they talked more, and looked at each other, and nodded and kept talking. He watched as Firefly and Cricket wavered and hopped their way back to the boat, where all three of them sat quietly on the deck.

★ ★ ★

Next morning Firefly and Cricket hid on a ready-to-burst milkweed pod next to the bus stop so that they could spy safely.

The front door of the giants' house opened, and Peter, wearing new orange sneakers, ambled out. The blue backpack was slung over his shoulders. The father and mother giants stood on the front porch and watched as he scuffed his way to the bus stop.

Jack's front door opened, and he ran down the road to where Peter stood waiting. He too was wearing a blue backpack. His mother and father giants joined the other giants on Peter's front porch, and all four of them waved.

From far off, down the driveway, down the giant road, around the bend of the woods, came the grinding sound of the school bus. The little creatures could feel its vibrations in the very air itself. Firefly couldn't take it any longer. Peter was standing right there, right next to them. They had to do something, didn't they? Say something? Were they just going to let him go?

"Come on, Cricket!"

And with that, Firefly ignored her sore wings and flew off toward Peter and Jack. Cricket's muscles gathered themselves again and

SPROING!

SPROING!

SPROING!

—he followed Firefly's flight until he landed a foot away from Peter, right on top of a dandelion. The dandelion swayed under his weight, and Cricket shifted from leg to leg, trying to keep his balance.

"Hey," said Firefly.

She floated back and forth in front of Peter, who was standing next to Jack. His blue backpack hung off his shoulders, and one shoelace of his new orange sneakers was already untied.

"Peter! Can you hear me?"

Cricket balanced on the dandelion and gathered his

strength for another leap. *LEAP!* And there he was, perched on Peter's orange sneaker. Cricket wrapped his two front legs around one of the eyelets and hung on grimly, braced for the slightest movement.

Grind.

The school bus was coming closer. But Peter didn't seem to hear them. Or see them. Look at Firefly, zigging and zagging right in front of his face, and he didn't even blink.

"Should I dive-bomb him?" she called down to Cricket.

From his precarious perch on the sneaker, Cricket nodded.

Firefly backed up in the air a few feet, spread her wings, and *zoom!* She flew straight at Peter's face. She bounced off his cheek and dropped a few inches in the air before she recovered herself.

Peter blinked. And then he turned to them and focused. Cricket leaped off the sneaker, back onto the milkweed pod, and Firefly did a midair flip. Peter held out his finger, and she alighted on it. He touched her wings very lightly.

"Good-bye, Firefly," he said.

The school bus was in sight now, lumbering around the bend of the woods. Now the bus was at the end of the long driveway. And then it wheezed to a halt right in front of them all.

The door whooshed open and blew Cricket right off the milkweed pod. He tumbled over and over, his carapace knocking against gravel and packed dirt, until he came to rest upright against the exposed root of the big maple tree. He cleared the dust from his eyes—everything was a blur—and when he could finally see again, he looked up—

—and Peter was gone.

Cricket leaped back up to his milkweed perch and watched Peter through the dusty bus windows as he and Jack made their way to a seat near the back. Firefly buzzed back and forth in the air above Cricket.

"Wait!" she called. "Wait!"

But the bus was so huge. So powerful. There was no way that even the fastest and bravest firefly in the history of the world could keep up with it.

SCRAPE.

Peter waved from behind the window.

"Are you coming back?" called Firefly.

He tilted his head as if he couldn't make out what she was saying.

"Do you promise?" she asked.

Peter put his hands around his mouth and started to call something. But the enormous engine roared into life again, drowning out his words, and then the bus lumbered off down the road, a cloud of dust in its wake.

CHAPTER THIRTY-THREE

A KINDRED SPIRIT

D o you think he's going to keep going to school?"
said Firefly.

Cricket pictured the morning just past, and
then he pictured tomorrow morning, and all the mornings to come. He pictured the door flying open, and Peter
running out, his blue backpack strapped to his back. He
pictured Jack running out of his own house down the
road, his own blue backpack slung over one shoulder.

"I think so," he said.

They looked at each other.

"Is he turning into a giant?" said Firefly.

"I don't know," said Cricket. "Maybe."

When the sun set that night, Vole lit a fire in the hearth, and Firefly and Cricket huddled next to it. The evening was crisp, and the leaves on the trees were turning to flame.

"Well?" said Vole.

"Well what?" said Firefly. "He went to school. If that's what you mean."

Vole leaned against the wooden table in the living room.

"He promised us he'd be back," said Firefly.

"He didn't, Firefly," said Cricket. "Not really."

The little creatures hunched sadly by the hearth. The firelight reflected off the hard shell of Cricket's carapace and glinted off Firefly's translucent wings. Vole looked over his furry shoulder at the paper boat on the wooden table.

"Vole, what's a kindred spirit?" said Firefly.

Vole tied a figure eight—the last knot on the list of sailor's knots—untied it, and tied it again before he spoke.

"A kindred spirit," said Vole, "is someone who understands the deepest dream of your heart."

Firefly floated along the ancient, brittle paper boat, brushing it lightly with one wing. Her deepest dream had been to fly to outer space, and Peter and Cricket and Vole understood this about her, didn't they? Even if they thought her dream was a little crazy, they understood her.

Cricket munched on tubers and fried fish. *A kindred spirit,* he thought. His deepest dream had been to be the first cricket Yogi Berra. Peter and Firefly and Vole understood this about him. Even if they thought his dream was a little crazy, they understood him.

"I have three kindred spirits," said Firefly.

"So do I," said Cricket.

"You're lucky, then," said Vole. "Kindred spirits are hard to come by."

"What about you, Vole?" said Cricket. "What's the deepest dream of your heart?"

Vole sat back in his chair, his paws moving automatically on his sailor knots. Firefly floated back and forth above the paper boat. Hungry, Cricket hunched over a leaf full of diced cattail tubers, his jaws grinding up and down. Look at them, these two little creatures. Look at how they had left behind their nations, ventured forth in search of their dreams.

"My deepest dream," said Vole, "is to carry out the destiny of the river vole. To sail down the river, to where the river meets the sea."

He looked down at the length of rope in his lap. Square knot. Figure eight. Bowline. Anchor hitch. Clove hitch. Rolling hitch. There were no other knots left to learn, no other sailing diagrams or star constellations left to decipher. He'd memorized the *River Vole's Guide*.

"But that's an easy dream," said Firefly. "Isn't it?"

Was it? Vole looked around his living room and his tiny galley. The shining knives, the scrubbed cutting board, the gleaming windows that looked out onto the dark, tumbling water of the river and the far side of the woods, invisible now. Firefly hovered just above Cricket, who leaned against the paper boat on Vole's dining table. If he left—if he actually did sail down the river, around the bend—he would miss these little creatures terribly.

He thought of the last night before last, when for the first time ever, he had cut the rope that bound the boat to the white birch and ventured away from the shore. Only to the middle of the river, where he dropped anchor, but still. He had felt the irresistible lure of the current beneath the boat, tugging him away from Firefly Hollow and everything he knew. Tugging him toward new places, places he had never seen. Tugging him toward adventure, and the life his ancestors had lived.

But his ancestors had not been alone. They had had

one another. They had been an entire nation unto them-selves. Vole looked at Firefly and Cricket, waiting for him to answer, and suddenly he spoke without thinking.

"You wouldn't want to come with me, would you?"

Then he looked down, afraid of what they would say. In his lap was the figure eight, perfectly tied.

"I would," said Firefly, and she did a flip.

"Me too," said Cricket, and he leaped right over the paper boat. Then he leaped back over again. Vole's heart filled with happiness.

"It's far from here," he cautioned them. "And I don't know the way, exactly."

"Neither do we," said Firefly.

"It'll be an adventure," said Cricket.

Firefly hoisted herself into the air and darted back and forth in front of the fireplace. She zoomed out the deck door and hovered in the air by the clump of tiger lilies. Cricket leaped out onto the deck too. Together they looked toward the giants' house. Peter was in there, asleep in his room. Were his blankets flung off? Were his hands clasped under his pillow?

"What do you think he's dreaming about?" said Cricket.

Firefly zigged back and forth, trailing light. Maybe Peter was dreaming of the getaway raft. Maybe he was dreaming of school.

"Maybe he's dreaming about us," she said.

CHAPTER THIRTY-FOUR

WHERE THE RIVER MEETS THE SEA

In the living room, the paper boat glimmered in the firelight. Vole looked at it and made up his mind.

"Cricket and Firefly, I need your help," he said. "Before we leave, I'm going to leave the boat at the giants' house."

"But why?" said Cricket. "It's your treasure."

"It was. But I don't need it anymore."

He untied the rope bridge and tossed it expertly into

the darkness. He had done it so many times that he knew exactly where the broken-off branch of the white birch was. The last rung of the bridge landed over it with a soft *whoosh*. Vole nudged the paper boat off the table and over to the bridge and watched as it tumbled awkwardly down to the ground.

Cricket and Firefly's dark eyes glowed in the night. Vole was bigger than the boat, but not by much. Firefly trailed along in the air just above him and Cricket leaped behind, both of them calling encouragement. It took all of Vole's considerable river vole strength to keep the boat moving, but he rolled and nudged it along with his paws.

In the darkness they made their way, by fits and starts and with breaks so that Vole could catch his breath, to the front porch of the giants' house.

"Step one," counted Cricket, as Vole heaved the heavy boat up the first step.

Firefly, her wings flapping, put her head underneath the bow and pushed as hard as she could, for moral support as much as anything else. Cricket braced all six legs and pushed up with his carapace.

"Step two," he panted.

Vole placed both paws on the boat and exerted all his strength for the last step.

"And . . . three!" said Cricket. "Done!"

They all stopped to catch their breath. Then Vole maneuvered the boat across the wide planks of the porch—a much easier task than shoving it up the steps—and set it on the welcome mat.

"A little more that way," said Cricket, "so that the door doesn't hit it when it opens."

When the boat was in just the right place, Vole brushed off his paws and leaned against the porch post.

"Vole?" said Firefly. "Tell us the truth. Will Peter really forget about us someday?"

"Boys grow into giants," said Vole.

That was all he said. But it was the same thing that the elders had been saying all along, and Cricket and

Firefly heard something in his voice, something true.

Cricket looked at the paper boat. There was something else he needed to know.

"Vole," he said. "Who was the boy who gave you the paper boat?"

"David," said Vole. "His name was David."

At that, Firefly slowed until she was a flicker of light in the dark air.

"But that's the father giant's name," said Firefly.

"I know," said Vole.

Cricket and Firefly were silent. This was a lot to think about, and when Vole turned back to the shore, they followed him. Then there came a sound from the giants' house, the sound of a window being pushed up. Peter's voice was faint but clear across the stretch of shore and path that separated his room from the little creatures on the beach.

"Firefly! Cricket! What are you doing?"

At the sound of his voice, Firefly and Cricket were off, leaping and flying back to the giants' house. Then Peter was at the kitchen window, the window where they had spent so many mornings waiting for him to emerge. He pushed up the screen and leaned out.

"What are you doing?" he said again.

Then, "Are you going away?"

They didn't say anything at first. Then Firefly nodded.

"We're going on an adventure," she said.

"Down the river," said Cricket.

"With Vole?" said the boy. "On the boat?"

"Yes."

Peter leaned out, looking at them. Wonder and confusion passed across his face.

"But I—I wouldn't fit," he said. "I can't go with you."

"We know," said Cricket.

"You can go to school, though," said Firefly. "And we can't."

"And you can play catch with Jack," said Cricket. "Real catch. Giant catch. And I can't."

"But what will I do without you?"

Cricket and Firefly didn't know what to say. The boy would be safe and warm inside his house, and inside the walls of his school. He would be with his new friend, the boy named Jack.

"Can't you wait for me?" said the boy. "Please?"

Again they said nothing. Then Firefly began to sing.

"Take me out to the river
Take me out to the sea.
Build me a raft and a mast and a sail
I don't care if I never get back."

She floated back and forth in the air, singing. Vole, who was down at the boat rolling up the twig bridge in preparation for cast-off, stood still and listened.

"I wish we could wait," said Cricket.

"But it's getting too cold," said Firefly, "and we have to go."

Vole leaned out over the rushing water.

"Ready?" he called.

He untied the mooring rope and half hauled up the anchor with a mighty heave. The boat bobbed out from the safety of the overhanging tiger lilies, anxious to join the current flowing south. Peter pressed his hands against the wire mesh of the window screen. Firefly brushed her wings against one hand. Cricket leaped up, one last time, and touched a wing to Peter's other hand.

Then they turned and made their way back to the shore, where Vole was waiting for them on the boat. The sun was just beginning to rise above the pine woods.

Maybe there would be crickets all along the journey, thought Cricket. Maybe the music of the southern crickets would be different, and beautiful. And before he lost his courage, he made a mighty leap onto the deck of the boat next to Vole.

Firefly flipped on her back and swept her gaze over the high heavens. Somewhere up there, invisible in the day, was Elder. *I'll be watching over you,* he had said. A wave of love poured through her. She swooped out over the river, and then she swooped back and hovered above Cricket on the deck.

The boat swayed into the middle of the river, as if it were dancing with the water. *When in doubt, use a bowline,* Vole recited to himself, his paws on the rudder. He needed to remember all the river vole lore in order to keep them safe.

"Cricket! Firefly!"

The little creatures both turned to the giants' house, where Peter now stood on the porch, the paper boat cradled in his hands, watching them. He cupped both hands around his mouth.

"Don't forget me," he called.

"We won't," called Firefly and Cricket together.

The sails puffed out white and full, and the boat began to pick up speed. Vole tugged the brim of his fishing cap lower against the breeze, and Cricket settled himself on a pile of rope and held on tight. Firefly let the wind blow her back and forth. Maybe, in the warm air currents of the south, she could learn some new aerial maneuvers, astonishing formations to teach the fireflies when they woke from their long sleep next spring. Maybe the great waters beyond, where the river met the sea, would sparkle with new fish, beautiful fish unfamiliar to Vole.

Maybe, thought Cricket, *I could find some treasure downstream to bring back for Gloria.*

The current was swift out in the middle of the river. From far upstream, the wind carried Peter's voice to them.

"Please," he called. "Please don't forget me."

"Never," called Firefly.

"Ever," echoed Cricket.

But they were too far away now, and their voices too small, for Peter to hear them. So Firefly did a loop-de-loop, and Cricket raised a wing, and then they waved and waved to the boy—to *their* boy—until the boat, with Vole at the helm, sailed around the bend and out of sight.

Firefly Hollow

About the Book

Cricket and Firefly are different from all the other crickets and fireflies—they have dreams for their lives. Because of this, they're seen as strange to the others in the hollow and are teased mercilessly, all because they aren't just like everybody else. When the two loners run away to meet the miniature giant who lives by the river, they commence on an adventure that may just lead to the fulfillment of their dreams. Young Peter, the miniature giant, can see and hear them, and he knows a thing or two about dreams as well, and sets about trying to help them reach theirs, as that might help him reach his own. And when they meet a river vole who is also yearning for something, they all ultimately learn that when you follow your dreams, no matter how crazy they might seem to others, life is full of unexpected possibilities.

Discussion Questions

1. How does Firefly and Elder's relationship begin? Why does Elder continue to protect and educate Firefly?

2. Why are Firefly's and Cricket's classmates so impatient with them? Why do they sometimes say mean things to them? How do their teachers respond both to Firefly and Cricket and the other students?

3. How does Gloria's accident affect Cricket? How does Cricket use her accident to help him persuade others to think like him?

4. Why is Vole the only river vole left on the river? What is Vole's dream? How does he work to achieve it?

5. How does Cricket's song bring him and Firefly together? What do they do the first night they meet?

6. What warning have the elders given Cricket and Firefly in regards to the giants? Why do Cricket and Firefly ignore the elders' warnings?

7. What does Peter do and say when he steps out of his house and meets Cricket and Firefly?

8. Why are Cricket, Firefly, and Vole so surprised when they meet? What do they learn about one another?

9. Why does Vole watch Cricket, Firefly, and Peter? What are Vole's observations and conclusions about the meeting?

10. Why does Vole catch the milk jug and place it on the rock where Peter will find it?

11. Why does Firefly practice her flying maneuvers every day? Why does she practice the parachute formation alone, away from all the other fireflies?

12. What prompts Cricket to run away from his home and from the other crickets? What is his plan?

13. Why does Firefly decide to leave Firefly Hollow? What secret does she tell that gets her in trouble? Why can't Elder come to her rescue?

14. Why do Peter's mother and father think Firefly and Cricket are imaginary? How do Cricket and Firefly react to this?

15. How do Firefly and Cricket meet Vole? What do Cricket and Firefly decide to do that night?

16. Why doesn't Peter want to return to school? What is his plan to avoid going? How do Peter's parents react to the news that he is not going to school?

17. How does Peter teach Cricket to catch? What is the first thing Cricket catches?

18. What does Peter learn about the afterlife from Cricket and Firefly? What happens to a cricket when it dies? What happens to a firefly?

19. What do Firefly and Cricket miss about their homes? As summer ends, what are Firefly's and Cricket's plans for the fall and winter?

20. How does Peter react to a new family moving in on his street? Who might have lived in the house before the new family?

21. When Firefly sneaks away from Cricket to return to Firefly Hollow, what does she overhear the other fireflies talking about? How does Firefly react?

22. Why do the crickets and fireflies leave their homes to talk to Vole? What do they learn about Cricket and Firefly?

23. What does Firefly see when she attempts to fly to the moon? How does it affect her flight?

24. How do Peter and Cricket help save Firefly? What happens when the raft sinks?

25. When Peter returns to school, what happens to his relationships with Firefly and Cricket?

26. What does Vole tell Cricket and Firefly about who his boy was? How do Cricket and Firefly react to that knowledge?

27. Why does Vole want to return the paper boat to his boy? Why doesn't he need it anymore?

28. Why do Cricket and Firefly decide to leave with Vole? How do they say good-bye to Peter?

Written to align with the Common core State Standards (corestandards.org), this guide has been approved by Simon & Schuster for classroom, library, and reading group use. It may be reproduced in its entirety or excerpted for these purposes.